DEATH BY EFFIGY

KAREN L. ABRAHAMSON

FOREWORD BY DANIEL HAND

GUARDBRIDGE BOOKS
ST ANDREWS, SCOTLAND

Published by Guardbridge Books,
St Andrews, Fife, United Kingdom.

http://guardbridgebooks.co.uk

Death by Effigy

ISBN: 978-1-911486-11-4

To Rhea who read the first draft and asked:
"It comes alive with the nats! You need more!"

And to Marcelle, my most trusted reader for so
many books and stories. Thank you.

FOREWORD

Burma has long held a position of significance in its region; its influence shaped by its location, traditions, and diversity. When Japanese forces entered Burma in early 1942, they set in motion a series of events that would, in a very real sense, decide the course of modern world history. The British Army, forced into the longest retreat of its existence, lost face in the eyes of its oriental subjects and so nudged the Empire into its slow, painful death; even reconquering the area in 1944-45 wasn't enough to restore British prestige. The Japanese wartime empire, though its brutality and privations achieved little else, paved the way for a post-colonial world.

This position of power, of wielding influence well beyond its own borders, has long been Burma's blessing—and its curse. A country the size of France, Burma lies at the crossroads between three great and conflicting-yet-undeniably-interrelated domains: India in the west, China in the north, and Southeast Asia in that direction. Throughout its history, this central location has bestowed on Burma a significance—cultural, economic and military—which it might otherwise have struggled to attain.

Nowadays, alas, when people in the West think of Burma (if they think of it at all) they tend to think despairingly of its troubled politics, its civil unrest, or its struggle with human rights. Any optimism tends to be associated with the efforts of Nobel Peace Prize laureate Aung San Suu Kyi; and even she can turn out to be disappointingly human on occasion. The country beyond the cameras, beyond the papers and the twenty-four hour news channels, is often tantalisingly out of reach.

Burma itself, with all its beauty and history and culture, remains largely forgotten.

In these enlightened times, this as a tragedy. A travesty. Because Burma, or Myanmar as it is now know, is a haunting, magical land, rich with astounding diversity, contrasts, and contradictions. Some of the world's great rivers flow only a few miles from some of the most rugged and hostile mountains; lush jungles enjoy year-round life, while the country's central belt can during the hottest months resemble nothing so much as a desert; the weather can go from relatively mild and pleasant to dangerously hot almost overnight, only then to give way to violent monsoons that lash the land for months on end; and the sprawling modernism of major cities clashes starkly with the bamboo villages that house huge swathes of the Burmese population.

More than this, the 'Burmese' people themselves are a veritable mosaic, each tribe and community wholly separate from—but inextricably linked to—those around them. Shans, Chins, Kachins, Karens, Nagas, Was, Mons,

Rohingya, Arakanese: the peripheral mountains and much of the coastline are positively saturated with these multifarious folk, each with their own traditions and beliefs and religions, leaving the main river valleys predominantly to the Bamar—the Burmans who give the country its name. It would be understating the issue to remark that these myriad ways of life have not always co-existed peacefully (nor do they yet), but the fact that they co-exist at all is what gives Burma its charm. With so much diversity enduring in so small a place, this mysterious world holds a mirror up to every facet of humanity—our relationship with the world, our relationship with the 'otherworld', our relationship with ourselves—with all the beauty and ugliness that might entail.

Any attempt to provide a brief overview of Burma, its history and culture, then, is bound to omit some (indeed, *most*) of the nuances of this very varied country. Even so, it is possible to strip the land and its peoples back to the barest essentials, allowing one at least a minor understanding of what it means to be of Burma.

~~~

In contrast to its neighbours China and India, whose written histories go as far back as one and a half millennia BC, Burma's documented history can only be traced to about 200 BC. Before that time, only archaeological remains provide clues as
~~~

to how Burma began.

From what we can tell, the country's earliest inhabitants settled in the dry central belt, alongside the Irrawady River. Their stone-, bronze- and iron-ages roughly matched the rest of Eurasia, and their artefacts reflect an affluent society with close trading ties to China and India. They were the first in the region—indeed, among the first in the world—to domesticate chickens and pigs, and to grow rice on an industrial scale.

Sometime in the second century BC, a people called the Pyu moved south into Burma from (we think) the area north of the Tibetan Plateau. The Pyu established a series of city-states, again predominantly on the central plains along the Irrawaddy, where their chiefs oversaw great developments in science, philosophy, and astronomy. These were, by some accounts, a peace-loving people, and their tenure lasted for the better part of a millennium. It was during this period that the country adopted Buddhism, probably imported from Indian trading colonies along the southern coastline. This deeply held faith would become a key ingredient in Burmese culture.

The Pyu era came to an end when yet another people, the Bamar, came from the north. They infiltrated the area slowly, albeit punctuated by deadly raids, so that by the mid-ninth century a fortress town called Pagan had grown strong enough to absorb weaker city-states. Two hundred years later, around the same time as William the Conqueror was making ready to seize the British Isles, another conqueror, Anawrahta, made ready to seize large swathes of territory from the frontier of what is now India all the way to the Straits of Malacca. Through the efforts of Anawrahta and his successors, Burma began to resemble the country it is today. This was Burma's golden age, when it stood as an economic and military powerhouse. Literature and poetry blossomed, and some of the most epic-scale temples and pagodas date from this period. More significantly in the longer term, this was when Burmese became the most commonly spoken language and Buddhism became the state religion.

After two and a half centuries, Burma's golden age came to an abrupt end when the Mongols, led by Kublai Khan, struck south and decimated the Pagan Empire. For the next three hundred years, from the mid-thirteenth to the sixteenth century, Burma was an anarchy of little kingdoms who fought relentless, small-scale wars. The disunity of today's various peoples had its seeds sown during these years of in-fighting.

This ended only in the 1530s, when Tabinshwehti's Toungoo Dynasty re-unifyied the land. It was the largest empire ever to have existed in Southeast Asia—though it might more correctly be thought of as a loose gathering of independent fiefdoms which happened to agree (however unwillingly) to operate as a single, unified body. In this, we can see much of modern Burma's mind-set: then, as now, the Shans, for example, would take issue with being called 'Burmese' (might as well call a Scot English!), though one might grudgingly admit a relationship, of some form, between the hill-folk and those on the plains. The fortunes of this empire ebbed and flowed, with subdued regions rebelling as soon as an opportunity presented itself. After 266 years, the Toungoo dynasty, like the Pagan before it, crumbled into mini kingdoms.

By now, new players were joining the story, though this time from the seas to the south rather than the mountain passes of the north: the Europeans. In 1511, the Portuguese established a trading station on the coast at Martaban. By the seventeenth century the Dutch, French, and British had also developed a half-hearted interest in this new and exotic world. Their curiosity, however, was tempered by the fact that the Burmese were too busy fighting each other to bother with commercial enterprise.

The final home-grown Burmese kingdom began its short existence in 1750, when a village-headman-turned-bandit, Alaungpaya, declared himself king and founded the Konbaung dynasty; within a decade he had re-unified the country—despite his enemies frequently being armed by the Europeans—and implemented reforms aimed at modernisation. The next hundred years saw a burgeoning culture of literature and theatre.

But the Konbaung was at its heart a militarist dynasty, and in this it was a victim of its own success. It expanded in all directions, and eventually found itself bordered with the recently conquered British India—and the British were never going to tolerate so aggressive and volatile a neighbour. Three wars, in 1824, 1852 and 1884, and resulting progressive annexations, left Burma with the official status of a province of India. The monarchy was abolished, as was the traditional link between religion and state: very quickly, 'Burma' ceased to exist, other than as the forgotten back end of an empire, thought of little by the government, far away in Westminster.

The Burmese did not make for compliant subjects. Time and again, protests and strikes and minor rebellions rocked the colony. Buddhist spiritual leaders, called *pongyis*, were often at the forefront of the unrest, incensed at the loss of their esteem and influence; the Burmese populace, indebted to Indian money-lenders and feeling like second-class citizens in their own country, eagerly followed their lead. The 'Burma Independence Army' that sprung up in the early days of the war against Japan was a natural continuation of these sentiments; from 1942 through the to the end of the war, these staunch Burmese nationalists went out of their way to cause headaches for both the British and the Japanese imperialists.

Burma was the scene of some of the most

violent actions of the Second World War—but it was a war fought between two foreign powers who, in the minds of the population, had no right being there at all. Burma belonged to the Burmese people; outside domination, no matter where it originated, was not welcome.

The Burmese gained their independence in 1948; and although their road has at time been rough, they are making their own way into the modern world.

~~~

This then, with many glaring omissions, is the history of Burma: a cycle of great leaps forward followed by several steps back; of rapid expansion followed by gradual decline, and almost ceaseless in-fighting.

If every land is a product of its history, it is not hard to discern why Burma today is what it is: fractured, at war with itself, but nevertheless fiercely protective of its own right to exist free of outside interference. Burma for the Burmese.

Perhaps the most defining characteristic of what it means to be Burmese is the country's intense dedication to the tenets of Buddhism. The search for *Dharma*, or truth, is at the heart of most Burmese lives—an outlook that has no place for either class or caste, and encourages every follower to be generous and kind to those around them. There are few peoples on this planet so wholly inclined towards charity as the Burmese:
~~~

to them, each act of aiding another takes them one step closer to *Nirvana*—total freedom from suffering and distress.

Beneath this Buddhist piety, however, lies a core of older folk-beliefs and superstitions. The Burmese never forgot the spirits and demons of their pre-Buddhist faiths, and to this day Burma's peculiar brand of Buddhism carries many folk elements such as astrology, alchemy, and animism. The planets, as well as impacting people's lives in much the same way as the western zodiac, can be malicious and baneful, and must be appeased through appropriate ritual; alchemy, beyond merely seeking to transform base metals into gold, also seeks eternal youth, so that an individual might live to see the arrival of the next Buddha; and every facet of life, from trees to hills to lakes to entire villages and districts, are possessed of spirits known as *Nats*, which might offer protection from evil, visit punishment upon transgressors, or simply bestow a blessing upon those who display appropriate obeisance. These *Nats* are led by a pantheon of thirty-seven 'official' Lords, which could very roughly be equated to saints (the vast majority, for example, met especially violent deaths, and are venerated as being holy subordinates of the Buddha); their tumultuous stories are frequently depicted in art and on stage. But *Nats* are not the only otherworldly beings with whom the Burmese must deal: in so mysterious a world, it is unsurprising that tales of demons and tricksters and terrible monsters should pervade Burmese culture. *Belu* ogres haunt the jungles and mountains; *Nāga* dragons swim through the earth; and a whole host of other creatures can either pose a threat or offer aid to those in need.

Perhaps the most potent symbol of this merging of Buddhism and animism can be found in Burma's famously religious landscape. The country is peppered with pagodas and stupas—any quick internet search will bring up dozens of pictures of these elegant stone structures poking out of the jungle like islands in a sea of green—in or around which the cremated remains of dead ancestors are buried. But these holy Buddhist grounds are very often guarded by pairs of *Chinthes*, dragon-headed lions said to represent a lion-shaped father slain by his own son, which can pounce on and devour Burma's enemies—a most un-Buddhist sentiment!

The Buddhist community, making up almost ninety per cent of the overall population, have always had a strained relationship with the various religious factions that make up the remaining ten per cent. Christian missionaries, arriving from Europe in the eighteenth century, made little progress in converting Buddhists to their cause, but enjoyed considerable success among the hill tribes along Burma's borders; the Rohingya, Burma's main Muslim community, have suffered decades of religious and cultural persecution (indeed, the Burmese government refuses to acknowledge their status as citizens); and the Burmese have never lost their hatred of Indian Hindus. Even those people who still practice Nat worship in its purest form, untouched by Buddhist influences, are looked down upon as backward. The social and cultural divide, so long an aspect of Burma's ethnic tapestry, has never fully disappeared; sadly, there are no signs that it will do so any time soon.

Much Burmese culture centres around festivals. Ostensibly 'merely' times of religious obeisance, these occasions long ago took on a separate significance, becoming great events for social, spiritual, and philosophical discourse. *Pwe*, or Pagoda Festivals, are regular, week-long, twenty-four-hour-a-day events that unite both city- and country communities in a spirit of excitement and celebration. Row upon row of stalls spring up around the pagoda, rich food and drink are constantly on offer, as are all types of wares that a passer-by might wish to purchase. And, of course, the entertainments. Music, dancing, dramatic performances: all are there to be seen, heard, and enjoyed.

Perhaps the most charming, the most culturally unique, the most *Burmese* of these entertainments, is the marionette play. The *Yoke-thei* ('Small Dolls') of a puppet troupe hold a significant, even vital, part in Burmese culture: for centuries, they were the only means of entertainment that could overcome the bounds of propriety which so dominated the actions of live performances. Being made of wood, none could take offense at their opulent dress, their sometimes blatantly political messages or—shock, horror!—their propensity for male and female characters to both share the stage *and touch*. In a country as naturally conservative as Burma, this freedom bestowed upon the marionettes and their masters a tremendous amount of power. Only on the puppet stage could the sentiments of the Burmese population be voiced to the King without fear of reprisal, and only on the puppet stage could news of current events, as well as educational material on subjects such as literature and history, be disseminated to that population without risk to their sensibilities. So, while the audience watched a *Belu* stalk through the jungle or a magician soaring through the sky, they could be confident that their ruler would receive their message, and that no punishment would be visited upon them for their impertinence; he likewise, knew that his propaganda was reaching the masses.

A beautiful Burmese custom—and a custom so beautifully Burmese.

~~~

And so, at last, to the book that you hold in your hand. <u>Death by Effigy</u> can rightly be compared to the romanticism posited by such historical figures as Rudyard Kipling and George Orwell who, though polar opposites in terms of
~~~

their stances on British imperialism, remained utterly charmed by this world throughout their lives. Like <u>Mandalay</u> and <u>Burmese Days</u>, this book is a love story, albeit a fantastical one, to the land and peoples of Burma: its traditions, its outlooks, its history.

Set during the Konbaung Dynasty, only years before the old Burma succumbs to the machinations of the British and Indian armies, the story perfectly encapsulates the mysterious, otherworldly nature that truly was Burma in the late-eighteenth/early-nineteenth centuries. The *Nats* and *Yoke-thei* at its heart, not to mention the sights, sounds, and smells it so beautifully evokes, sing of Burmese magic. Here is a Burma that Alaungpaya himself would recognise.

In a world so aware of its myriad lands and peoples, and yet so implacably divided in spite of this self-awareness, we could do with more books like this: stories that take the 'other' and embrace it, rather than pushing it away. Karen L. Abrahamson has done us all a great service in opening the door to one of our most forgotten cultures, and one can only hope that others will follow her lead.

—Daniel Hand
Author and Historian

DEATH BY EFFIGY

Chapter 1

The renowned troupe of thirty-seven nat-imbued puppets usually came once a year to play for the Lord of the White Elephant and living Bodhisattva that was mighty King Bodawpaya of all of blessed Burma. But this year, soldiers had come to the troupe halfway through their winding travels through the southern provinces of recently conquered Arakan and, to Aung Aung the puppet singer's surprise, demanded that they turn northward again. They were commanded to perform before another of the king's many marriages—a traditional performance intended to appease the Great Nats and bring good luck to the marriage.

Apparently the king did not see the contradictions in his actions.

A long journey on a soldier's barge up through the heart of the parched country had deposited Aung Aung and the troupe in their usual dwelling in the mile-wide walled Royal Enclosure in the ancient city of Amarapura. This time, however, it did not feel like a pleasure to be kept within those walls. This time, with every breath Aung Aung took, the place felt entrapping and dangerous.

And such danger required the utmost care in seeking the Great Nats' blessings, for the spirits of Burma, both great and small, were a perverse, unruly lot who could bring great riches or cause a great fall.

The time before the rains had left the narrow streets of Amarapura heavy with red dust and oxen dung. The steep peaked roofs of the stilted teak buildings were pounded by the hammer-weight of the sun, while the people were somnolent and sullen and given to uncharacteristic temper. The streets rang with mutters and angry voices. Dust dulled the bright blues and reds of the silk and cotton threads hung to dry in the weaver streets and stained the white sides of the spires and temples—even within the king's compound. At least that was how it looked to an old man's failing eyes, and at sixty-five, Aung Aung was considered very old.

Along the mighty Ayerawady River, the fishing fleet's blue and white sails hung flaccid, so men took to oars that creaked like old joints. The markets reeked of drying fish and river shrimp and the stench of rotting mango and jack fruit. The Buddhist temple bells hung silent on the silver and gold pagodas, and in the early morning even the silent processions of begging, saffron-robed monks moved slower. At every street corner and in every house, sweet incense coiled around unsanctioned *nat kadaw*—spirit shrines that the king had ordered pulled down but that had quietly reappeared given the long drought.

Everything waited for the monsoon. Everyone prayed to Buddha. Those brave enough to defy the king prayed quietly to Min Mahagiri, the ancient king of the Nats and to Boun Magyi, the Rice Mother, but the old spirits, and Buddha, apparently all turned away. Or perhaps it was the Nats' retaliation against the king's command that only Buddha be worshipped.

Aung bent his head to the floor in prayer beneath the offering he had placed on a shelf high up on the central post of the guesthouse where the Great Nat could watch over those who dwelt here. The stilted building with the ornately carved teak lintels stood six feet above the ground on wooden posts to create cool shade and shifting air underneath. Inside it had high, dimly lit ceilings with a single large room and raised platforms that provided sleeping space, though in this heat, the troupe and the puppets slept on the cooler ground below the floor.

In the market he had taken great care in choosing the most perfect coconut. He had placed it on a banana leaf along with fresh bananas and rice and perfect green betel leaves. Everything was precisely as it should be, so surely if he completed his prayer the drought that had only become worse as the troupe travelled north would break and the troupe would be safe through their perilous performance of songs that highlighted the foibles of the nobles. With the rains the people would return to being the smiling children of Buddha as the king insisted. Of course, whether they truly the embraced the king's edict against the nats was a matter of speculation, for there were many faiths in Burma and the nats were most ancient of all.

From beneath the floor came the low-pitched voices of the puppeteers interspersed with the lilting voices of the *yoke thei*—the puppets.

"Great Min Mahagiri, King of the Nats and keeper of households," he prayed, giving voice to his carefully prepared bargain, "Accept this offering from your faithful servants. Always we celebrate your greatness in our tales, My Lord. But the people and the land are sick and starving for lack of water. May we honor you and please you however you desire so that you bring the rains and save the lives of those who depend upon you. Please hear my words, oh, great Min Mahagiri, keep safe your faithful servants of the..."

"Murder! Murderer!" A wail came through the floorboards.

Aung jerked upright, his prayer forgotten. Such a sound could only mean that disaster had found them. His offering was too little and far too late.

"Aung, we need you." U Winna appeared on the ladder in the doorway.

Aung struggled to stand, but his old legs cramped from kneeling.

The manager of the troupe, U Winna, was a

little round-headed man whose *paso*, the plaid sarong that all men wore, always looked wrinkled and unkempt, in sharp juxtaposition to his keen mind for business. He had a jolly round belly that spoke of the troupe's good fortune, but right now lines of strain framed his dark eyes. Aung had last seen that look in Arakan when U Winna first learned that King Bodawpaya's marriage was to his own thirteen-year-old daughter, youngest of his children.

U Winna's black eyes flitted from Aung to the offering and narrowed in disapproval.

"Damnation, Aung! Are you trying to get us all arrested? Propitiating a nat in the king's enclosure! He might turn a blind eye to what happens in his city, but he surely will not here. I told you this morning, let the peasants make their offerings. That is surely enough." He nodded as if to himself. "Not that any offering does much good. I've begun to think the king's right—in the matter of the nats at least. Maybe the Great Nats don't exist and this drought is just weather." He fanned himself in vain. "This heat is enough to kill a man."

"What's happened below?" Aung asked. He ignored U Winna's insult to the Great Nats for the wails and cries of dismay continued from the space underneath the floor. It was unlike the man, but something was clearly wrong.

U Winna shook his head. "Another disaster I should have foreseen."

Such hopelessness. U Winna knew the

marriage was inevitable once the king saw the girl's beauty. U Winna had accepted that inevitability, even though he would never see his favorite child again once she joined the royal court. But a new worry clogged his voice.

Aung stilled the wobble in his rickety legs and straightened his blue plaid paso and white Indian tunic. On his head he wore a loose turban that the sunlight had faded almost as grey as the few remaining strands of his hair. Age had crept into his life like a slow flood over the past few years. At first it had been like a bit of unfortunate rain on a performance. His hips had ached. His finger joints had thickened. Had he been a puppeteer, he should have been forced to retire. His hands had never had the fine skills so enjoyed by Saya Lin, the master puppeteer, but now they challenged him just to hold a spoon to his mouth, and what had once been a long stride had become an old man's shuffle.

"I ask again, what has happened? What is that noise?" The offending wails had been replaced by loud voices and female moans of grief.

"Leave your useless offerings and see."

"You may know business, U Winna, but I know the spirits and their appeasement. They are at work here. Can you not feel it? The air carries their tang and says they are unhappy. I simply seek Min Mahagiri's assurances that the rains will come and ill winds will pass us by."

"Well your offerings have been for naught!

Our doom is upon us!"

The portly man disappeared down the house ladder. Aung bowed once more to the coconut head of watchful Min Mahagiri before he climbed down into the unrelenting afternoon sun.

In the blessed shade beneath the teak structure the air was cool as a young girl's touch. The shadows, however, blinded his old man's eyes. Another faculty eaten away by the naga-dragon of time. Indeed, at times it felt like the naga of years weighted each of his arms and legs and snaked inside his brain.

"Aah, there you are, Master." Young Thura, his apprentice singer appeared out of the mass of troupe members crowded around the yoke thei's wicker trunks. He was a handsome youngster of seventeen with the taller, thin build of the Chin hill tribes. Normally his heritage would have disqualified him from apprenticeship, but Aung had heard him sing at six years old. Aung had demanded U Winna allow an exception, so that the boy-child Thura had been raised by Aung. Between the two of them they sang the voices of all the puppets and the songs of social commentary they were famous for.

But now something clearly was wrong. Thura looked close to crying, although such extreme emotion was against the tradition of Burmese equanimity known as *bhammasan chin*. The problem was clearly not with the musicians who stood worriedly to one side, inspecting the large circle of gongs and the huge dragon drum for imperfections.

No, it was the puppeteers: they crowded around their precious yoke thei and their baskets like mother tigers with their young. The yoke thei, the small spirit-inhabited puppets, were the troupe's stars. The fact that they were nat-inhabited was a secret only the troupe shared. There was the votaress in her crimson *longyi*-sarong on her knees praying fervently to the Great Nats. The small alchemist waved his wand and cast luck incantations—to no avail apparently. The puppet king's ministers were huddled together, their silver and sapphire decorated pasos and vests glinting as they murmured. Clad in cream silk, gold and pearls, Minthamee, the princess puppet, clung, sobbing, to her prince, the Mintha. Beside them, on her knees, Minthamee's handmaiden wailed, and Yamin, the page, danced on one foot making funny faces, apparently trying to make the princess smile. The naga hissed, the garuda-bird ruffled his green-gold feathers and beat his human chest, the white horse reared, and the monkey king hung from the floorboards above them shaking his fist.

Aung's mouth went dry. His tongue felt too large, for clearly something horrible had happened amongst the puppets—and disaster for the living yoke thei was disaster for them all.

"What has happened?" he asked.

No one answered.

"What has happened?" he demanded, projecting his voice as if he was in a performance that would hold and mesmerize his audience.

The handmaid's wail stopped. The ministers looked up from their huddle. Minthamee wiped her eyes on a handkerchief the Mintha offered, and the white horse stopped his whinnying and pawed the wicker of his basket. Yamin stuck out his tongue. Zeya, the apprentice puppeteer, Saya Lin, the String Master, and all the others who danced the puppets turned to Aung. Old Saya Lin, a thin man with spidery arms full of the sinew of long years of working the strings, looked as grey as his thick head of hair. His eyes were filled with unspilled tears and his face was almost slack with unfathomable disaster.

Aung stepped up and caught Saya Lin's hand. "Old friend, we have travelled far and given many performances together over the long years. Never have I seen you look so far removed from your *bhammasan chin*. I repeat: what has happened?"

Saya Lin swallowed and closed his eyes. Around them a hubbub of voices exploded in the shadows under the house as everyone tried to explain. He heard 'puppet' and 'knife' and 'Min' until finally he raised his hands.

"Silence!" he roared with the voice he reserved for the king puppet, Min. He turned back to his friend. "Saya Lin, old friend, please speak to me."

Saya Lin's mouth worked as if he had no tongue. Finally he turned and waved the puppeteers apart, creating a path between Aung and the puppets' baskets. U Winna stood to one side, his arms crossed on his chest.

He motioned Aung forward.

The wicker chests contained the riches of the troupe, the thirty-seven finely crafted and bejeweled yoke thei—when the small spirit-inhabited creatures were unanimated, or sleeping in their wood. Now they clearly were not sleeping or in their wood, instead they were out of their baskets in their spirit-animated state. The small doll marionettes had been commissioned centuries ago by royal decree. These puppets, and the troupe, were the only performers in the land that could perform elevated above the level of King Bodawpaya's head. They were also the only source of news and critique of an increasingly despotic king, his functionaries and nobles, in a country they tightly controlled.

Not surprisingly, given the animated state of the puppets, the tops were off the wicker baskets, exposing the fine silken beds where puppets slept. All the baskets were empty. All but one.

That basket was traditionally kept to itself as a sign of respect. A cold wind rushed through the stilts that supported the house and turned Aung's skin to gooseflesh.

Min, the king, lay with his small jointed arms outstretched like a human body tossed aside by the Gods. His head, separated from his body, lay skewed to one side and split open to expose the sweet-scent Yamani wood inside.

Aung's legs started to give, but he waved away Thura's offer of a stool. He inhaled deeply, knowing this was what he had been dreading since they arrived.

"How could this have happened?" he asked softly, studying the small murder victim's body.

"Well I, for one, would say that the humans failed in their duty. Clearly *that's* what happened," said Yamin, the cheeky little page.

"Can't you see the humans are as horrified as we are?" Prince Mintha said.

It was unfathomable that this could happen. The yoke thei were the puppeteer's children. They bathed when the troupe bathed. They ate when the troupe ate and were carefully locked away to sleep when the troupe slept. That someone would kill one of the beloved figures was almost unbelievable. That the victim should be the Min was utterly terrifying.

He turned back to the bent grieving heads of the puppeteers. "Well? You were here, were you not? The yoke thei are never to be left unattended."

Saya Lin shuffled his feet, raising a small cloud of dust. "Last evening, Aung. When you were at your rest and U Winna was attending to the troupe's business, we were invited to a performance of the royal musicians at the *pwe* festival."

"Yes, yes." That was the usual way of things in the royal enclosure. Performance after performance, delegation after delegation, even from the tall, black-clad foreigners who wandered the country preaching against Buddha and the nats and teaching of a different god.

The puppeteers shuffled uneasily.

"You mean to tell me that you abandoned our children?"

"You were here, old man! Did you hear nothing?" yelled Htain Thaunt, a puppeteer of forty.

Aung closed his eyes, for it was true. "I slept, and for once I slept without waking. My ears are not as they used to be." But was that true? Had he not, when he roused to relieve his old man's bladder, heard something and chosen to believe it was nothing?

"What shall we do, Master? We cannot perform without Min. The king will expect his effigy on stage. He'll expect the songs you wrote to his sexual prowess," Thura said.

"A pox on your songs." Yamin leapt across the tops of the baskets to face Aung from the rim of the Min's basket. "What about us? We are 37, not 36. We are from a single tree and now one of our branches is taken." He was a small boy, barely eighteen inches tall and dressing in silken blue pantaloons that ended at his knees and a colorful vest with small golden tassels for decoration. His long dark hair was caught in two pony tails high on either side of the crown of his head and, like all the puppets, his strings were a small neat bundle that sat like a pack between his shoulders. He had a jolly little round face that, at the moment, scowled.

"All true, Yamin. All too true." All part of the disaster. King Bodawpaya was their patron and he had commanded their performance. To not perform would be disaster for the troupe and a crime against the king. Clearly someone had brought this disaster upon them.

He motioned to Thura for a stool and his joints creaked and popped as he sank down. "Perhaps there is a way we could still perform. I could change my song. We could place a curtained bower upon the stage so no one would see the Min."

The little page leapt down to face Aung.

"What about my questions?"

Aung ignored the child-like puppet, his thoughts consumed with permutations that might still save them, but…. He looked up at the Master puppeteer, Saya Lin. "It can be done or something can, but think: If someone would destroy the puppet, what more would they do to stop our performance? We must find the culprit and quickly."

"But who would want to do such a thing and why?" Yamin asked.

"That is a very good question, little master," Aung said, nodding down to the page. "The troupe has been absent from Amarapura for many months. I cannot believe someone would hold a grudge against any of our members for so long."

But over the years there had been enemies made. Other puppet troupes that wished royal patronage, but Saya Lin's skills had held preeminence for forty years. Their precious puppets were the best; as far as they knew the only set made in the old ways and carved from a single Yamani tree so that the wood nat still dwelt within the set as if they remained one body. To destroy the Min effectively ruined the whole puppet troupe and silenced Aung's cutting songs which gave the people their only voice at the royal court.

He looked up at Saya Lin. "If this is truly an attempt to stop our songs, then I can think of only one man who would want to stop our performance." He peered beyond the tearful puppeteers, the worried musicians and his own apprentice, but there were no other ears to hear his pronouncement.

"The king himself," he whispered and heard the shocked intake of breath. "He could have ordered a servant to do it. He could even have arranged the musical performance to lure you all away."

He looked around at the troupe, young and old. Their lives depended upon the performance, for Bodawpaya did not take kindly to anything that stood in the way of his desires. The man was a despot with too many crimes to enumerate. Out of self-preservation, most citizens turned a blind eye to them, but the troupe's very purpose was, under the guise of entertainment, to rub the king's face in the dung of his court's actions—in a humorous way, of course. On occasion, the troupe's performances had even helped right wrongs—like the time a noble's confiscation of lands from a town had been revealed to the king through a performance where the offending puppet had eaten so much he exploded while the starving villagers had looked on. It had been a wonder of Saya Lin's puppet magic that they had managed to have one of the nobles 'explode' after gorging, and yet not damage the puppet underneath. The king had returned the land to the people.

But perhaps Bodawpaya had tired of being reminded of his, and his court's, failings. On the other hand, could not the king simply order the troupe arrested if he was tired with their songs? He would not need a real excuse.

"Saya Lin, you and the others: you must find out who was near our house yesterday evening. Perhaps one or two of the most subtle questioners can be assigned the task. Definitely not you, Thura. You are only my apprentice. Or you either, Yamin!" he motioned to his apprentice who was already easing towards the edge of the earth-scented shadows and to Yamin scampering toward the freedom of the gardens. The lad was too hot-headed and unsubtle, while Yamin was, well, a nat-inhabited doll that no one beyond the puppet troupe knew existed. It would not do for him to be running loose—at all!

"Saya Lin, you choose. Whoever it is must be

discreet. We do not want word of this getting back to the king, do you hear? The rest of you must remain here and fix that puppet as best you can. Check all the others as well. And the instruments. And make sure our equipment is not left unattended. We cannot afford further sabotage."

Aung struggled to his feet. "In the meantime I think I shall take a walk. I need to think on this."

CHAPTER 2

Caught by the old singer's words, Yamin toed the sun-heated soil and considered how he might go in search of the culprit regardless of what the old man said. It was most unfair that they had stopped him. He might be small, but he was very good at sneaking into places unseen. At least he thought he would be. The very fact that he was small worked in his favor. That he had not had a chance to prove himself previously was not his fault.

Around him the puppeteer's camp was a hubbub of activity as various puppeteers volunteered to seek information. They didn't even think of asking the yoke thei and yet it was a yoke thei who had been killed. If, like he said, they'd been *paying attention* like they were supposed to, this wouldn't have happened.

And now they weren't paying attention again. At least not to him.

Perhaps this time it was a good thing.

The old singer had gone and Princess Minthamee was still clinging to the Mintha. She didn't seem the least inclined to call for his performance.

Which meant…

A cautious step towards the larger world beyond the bushes around the guesthouse. A look out of the corner of his eye to see if anyone was watching.

And there was the perfect branch to duck underneath. Perhaps if he hurried he could catch up to the old singer. At least then he could learn what the old man learned and keep the old human honest.

The leaves barely rustled as he stepped into their shadows.

~~~

Stepping out of the house's shadow was like stepping onto Min Mahagiri's anvil. The Great Nat King had been a human blacksmith before he was killed by a king and became the patron of every house in Burma. Even in the shadows of the teak and tulip trees the sun found Aung's head and shoulders and forced his hunch a little deeper. The usually green grasses of the king's enclosure were a heated brittle brown—except near the small streams that flowed between the trees—and even those channels were nearly dry. The small bells on the lintels and peaks of the noble houses barely moved and left the air barren of their usually fluid music. Hard blue sky stretched overhead like a downturned bowl, but in the distant south, beyond the Sagaing Hills, towered the huge clouds that came with the heat. When enough of them formed surely it would bring the rains and cooling winds
~~~

and the mud and the blessed planting of this year's rice. He prayed it was so. It could not come soon enough.

The royal enclosure stood behind solid stone walls as tall as two men, with spiral towers for the guards spaced along its length. Beyond the walls the denizens of bustling Amarapura would be going about their business, trading the blood-red rubies and golden teak of the north for the goods brought upriver from Yangoon and the coast. The streets would be alive with the bright blue, green, and pink longyi, paso, and headgear of the people of the provinces, the swaying gold-tasseled palanquins of the nobles. Even this late in the day the markets would be alive with mud-scented fishermen from the river, cloth sellers, and farmers selling their fresh meat, the last of the rice, and what should be lush perfumed mango and honey-sweet jack fruit. This year the fruit was badly stunted from lack of water. The air would be smoky from the cooking fires braising pork or fish. The voices of the vendors would rise and fall in sing-song; the small food stalls would sell pungent curry and deep fried river minnows that would crunch nicely in your teeth.

His stomach growled.

Unlike the lively city, the walled royal enclosure lay sedate and quiet. The tall teak palaces scattered through the trees housed the nobles and their wives after the king ordered them to leave their palaces throughout the country to deter the specter of local uprisings. The sound of music, the soft wail of the *hne,* wafted out the windows of the Number One Queen's palace, close by the king's abode. Farther on lay the lesser queens' home and there he paused at the sound of soft voices and crying, but there was no one visible beyond the massive bushes of pink bougainvillea.

Odd, when there should be excitement radiating from the palace and the bustle of the preparation for another wife. He caught the unfriendly regard of a guardsman at the main entrance and shuffled on. His faded longyi and turban marked him as a common man to be met with suspicion before he was recognized by those who had been at the palace long enough to remember him. But many of the old familiar faces did not seem to be around this time. Perhaps the stories were true about the king sending more soldiers to Manipur to augment his cousin's garrisons against the English foreigners.

The house he sought was that of the king's vizier, that vaunted man who wore a silver headdress and walked under a tiered umbrella only slightly less impressive than the king's. Aung shuffled around the side of the palace until he reached the smaller building that housed the vizier's servants where his old friend Daw Ma Sanda worked. He ducked under the raised floor to the shadows and the bustle of the women working there.

"Aung? Is it truly you come back so soon?"

Daw Ma Sanda emerged from the shadows. "But of course it is. He sent for you." She smoothed her deep blue longyi and placed her hands upon her slim hips as she frowned. "And it has taken you three days to come to see me."

"Only because I had to prepare myself for your loveliness." He smiled and bowed, his hands brought together at his breast.

Daw Ma Sanda came from the same town as Aung. As a young woman she had been a beauty, and he had once thought he might marry her, but then he had apprenticed as a puppet singer and had travelled too long with his troupe. When he came back a year later she was gone—a lesser wife of a passing noble. The noble had long since died, and with her age, she was reduced to being a servant for the vizier. And so all these years later, they had rekindled their relationship—or what relationship the old were allowed to have.

Daw Ma Sanda bowed in return, her pressed palms at her head in a show of respect. Then she burst out laughing, her sun-browned skin crinkling around her brown eyes.

"You old fool. How are you? Still walking, I see."

"Was there any doubt?"

She shrugged, still graceful even at her advanced age, her hair still thick and dark on her head. "Perhaps, but I prefer my old men to also see the light. It proves there's still life and hope."

A strange thing to say and stranger still when

she caught his arm and led him back out to the shadows and under the trees. She smelled of rice water and the sweetness of female sweat—still just as he had dreamt of in his youth.

"You are still beautiful, you know." Aung told the truth, for her youthful beauty still shone through in the silkiness of her hair that she kept confined in a neat twist at the back of her head and in the fineness of her features under the white *thannaka* paste she used to protect her skin from the sun. She pulled him to a stop beside one of the streams, but the lack of rain had reduced the water to a thread of silver amid a rocky bottom. The water nats were far away, playing in the Ayerawady River, and it left the waterway barren.

"And you are a blind old man if you think so. I suppose there is a reason our sight goes as we age—you cannot see the wrinkles. How are you Aung? I've been worried." Her dark eyes met his. She crossed her arms as if to protect herself and him, too, and he noticed a small wooden cross on a leather thong at her neck.

"Why worried? I am well." But perhaps she had heard something that would be a clue to what had happened.

Daw Ma Sanda cast a glance back at the house and then through the trees as if she did not want anyone to overhear. "There have been rumors, Aung. The songs you sing—the king grows tired of your barbs. It ruins his humor and makes life difficult for all, or at least that is what my Master says."

Aung nodded. "Tell me more."

"He says that the country teeters on the brink of another war and have we not just recovered from our futile battles with Siam? Not to mention dealing with Arakan? He worries that your troupe's blunt words may tip Bodawpaya over the edge and he will do more than send troops into Manipur. What would happen if he declared war on the English in India?"

She must have read something on his face as he considered her words. "What is it? Has something happened? Something has!" Her hands came up and cupped his face in the uncharacteristic intimacy that only the aged and the very young were allowed. "Please. You know I am your ally."

Aung shook himself loose and wished for a stool, for what had happened was a burden that drained an old man of strength. Did he dare tell Daw Ma Sanda what had happened? If word reached the king that the yoke thei were less than perfect, they would not be allowed to perform, and their patronage could be withdrawn. No one would be left to sing the songs of the king's misbehaviors and their leaders' failings. There was no question that, after all Aung's years of ridicule, he and the troupe would disappear at the pleasure of the king. While at his age he would not protest the end of an overlong life, the troupe would also likely bear the king's wrath for allowing the puppets to be damaged.

He looked into Daw Ma Sanda's dark eyes. "There has been sabotage to the troupe. Beyond that I dare not say. We are investigating." He caught her hands. "Tell me what you know. Tell me all the rumors you've heard."

"Rumors?" She shrugged prettily, like a school girl, and the hard sunlight caught on the silver strands that he had not noticed in her hair. "Is it a rumor when my Master speaks of how, after news reached the king of your latest song, the king smashed a favorite celadon pot, a pot that was the spoils of his ancestor's wars with Siam?"

Aung drew in a tired breath and felt like the shrunken stream. The song was a good one. One of his most clever. It was Thura's brilliant idea when he heard of the king's pending marriage to a child who could be his great granddaughter. "But how could he have heard? I have only sung it within the troupe? I'd planned to unveil it at the wedding *pwe*—the festival."

Daw Ma Sanda snorted. "Trust you to ridicule old Bodawpaya's sexual prowess on the very wedding day when he must prove it. The girl will need to be an *apsara* herself if she hopes to get that old man up to business. God's will, I suppose." She crossed herself.

Her bawdy humor might have surprised him, but her gesture surprised him more.

He raised his hand to touch her small cross. "When did this happen?"

"This?" Her hand closed protectively around the Christian cross and her eyes closed so she lost her worried look. "I found God a year ago, just after you last left. I had been speaking to the priests in the city, or rather they would speak to me and it seemed that they made sense—far more than the lie of spirits inhabiting the trees and creeks. At least the king had it right when he banned that heathen belief. And God gives me peace in my old age when life does not. He cares for me, when all Buddha says is to accept that life is suffering." Her eyes opened and searched his. "Perhaps you would like to join me? Renounce the spirits and Buddha for the true God? We go to burn a spirit shrine tomorrow. You could come."

Aung swallowed back his revulsion at the act for he needed her information. There was no way he would renounce the spirits when he lived with them every day in the form of the yoke thei. How could Daw Ma Sanda have strayed so far from the woman he remembered? He had not expected this—at all.

He found a smile. "Thank you, but I fear I must spend my time rooting out who plots against my troupe. There are only a few days before the marriage pwe. It is odd that Bodawpaya would marry one so young, but according to her father, the girl is a great beauty. But for a common girl to marry a king—I would never have thought it."

Shaking her head, Daw Ma Sanda leaned in close. "That is the thing. Bodawpaya is also like a child these days. He has the temper of a five-year-old and in his fits will destroy what annoys him. The entire court trembles when he has one of his tempers and there are rumors that Prince Bagyidaw may lead the nobles against him, but I am not so sure he is that brave. I am afraid for you, Aung. Could you perhaps, rewrite your song? Remove its teeth?"

He looked at her in horror. "Would you silence us, then? Just as he would? Make us his creatures just like his feckless courtiers?" He waved his hand at the palaces surrounding them amongst the trees. The sun fell ferociously on his head and shoulders. Something roared in his ears and his vision darkened.

"Aung!"

She caught his arm before he fell and helped him settle beside the stream. Then she palmed the sun-warmed water onto his head and shoulders. The evaporation helped a little. He regained himself.

"I'm sorry, Aung. Who was I to even suggest such a thing? It would be against your very nature. You have always spoken the truth—as you know it." Her hand touched her cross again. "I remember when we were children and you told me that you intended to marry me. But then you went away and my future husband came to marry me and I told myself you had only joked." She hung her head. "Inside I always knew you spoke the truth."

She sat beside him, so thin and proud and

sad, and he remembered her too well from those days long ago and the horror he had felt when he returned for her and she was not there. But that was how it was done—marriages arranged and approved and the young people involved went along. After all, no one had known of their words together. Arrangements between a young man and woman simply were not done.

"Funny how life brings us back together again," she said and leaned in and placed a soft kiss on his cheek. "Perhaps the true God finally heard our prayers now that one of us directs their prayers to him."

He shivered. All those years the nats had not listened and now he felt their brooding darkness all around, like the scent of durian or fresh blood through the trees. Sometimes the nats of this world were just like carrion birds circling. Daw Ma Sanda might choose to be blind to the older powers of the world, but he was not.

"It may be karma that brings us together now, but it will be for a very short time if the troupe does not perform. Tell me, what of the other rumors in the palace? A wedding always brings many of them, does it not?" And Daw Ma Sanda would be the one to tell them. She was always keenly eared for the nuggets of truth from amongst the chaff of the palace's daily conversation.

She looked thoughtful a moment and then focused on him.

And smiled. "There are so many. This place," she waved at the enclosure, "is like a city or country unto itself with all its spies and petty politics."

"Tell me."

"Well, the old queen is furious with the king for this wedding. She fumes at him that he is a ridiculous old man who is like this." She held up a hand, one little finger drooping, and cackled her humor, then stretched out her feet and dabbled them in the creek water like a much younger girl. "Bagyidaw, her grandson and the crown prince, has told her that her tantrums are not befitting her station, but apparently she does not listen. Her grandson is not pleased with her, but he defends her to his grandfather when the king threatens to have her poisoned." She chuckled again and leaned against his shoulder. "Sometimes I swear they are here strictly for our entertainment."

"Except that they can be deadly." He placed an arm around her shoulders and an old candle he'd almost forgotten flared and sputtered in his heart. She still fit him physically, if no longer in faith. "What else is there to know?"

"One of the girls who cooks for the lesser queens has been carrying notes for the new girl. It has the kitchen women aflutter with rumors that perhaps she is not a virgin—not that that would matter to Bodawpaya. There are soldiers betting the odds of whether the king will even be able to father a child upon her. Now would that not be a sad life—to be married and never know the bedroom pleasures? Unless of course...." She nudged him bawdily with her elbow.

"You mean she may have a lover in the town even now? She is only thirteen!"

Daw Ma Sanda waggled her eyebrows.

He would need to speak to U Winna. Could it be possible? U Winna would be horrified. The little man had been acting odd ever since news of his daughter's elevated marriage reached them. One moment puffed up as a peacock, the next deflated as a pig's gallbladder.

"From what I hear," she continued, "there were many messages, but I do not know to whom. Are you saying this may relate to your sabotage?" She splashed her feet in the rill of water again. "This really is a pleasure. You should try it."

He did, stretching his hoary old feet with the long twisted toes in beside her plump ones. His looked like giant feet, or the roots of a tree, beside her much neater ones, but the water did feel good.

"I'm not sure how it relates, but any information is helpful now."

She turned to look him straight on. "If any of this turns up in your songs they'll know who it came from. There are people in my master's household who will report our discussion."

He shook his head and squeezed her hand. "Don't worry. I won't sing about it."

She tossed her head as if her long hair was loose. "There are also stories about the foreigners.

There are some on the coast who wish to visit with the king. Bodawpaya is upset that these same foreigners fight against his cousin in Manipur and help the rebels in Arakan. He does not wish to have them near his court for fear of spies." She looked down at her hands. "What would we do if something was to end king Bodawpaya's rule?"

She sounded suddenly old and worried and he pulled her into his side. She felt soft and vulnerable and thinner than he remembered as a girl, but then age had melted flesh off of him, too.

He stroked her hair. "You are still young enough you would move to the new king's palace." When a new king was crowned, in a show of wasteful excess, he abandoned the past king's royal city and moved the entire court to a new location of his choosing. The area around Amarapura was littered with the walls of such abandoned royal cities, and their temples. The palaces themselves were either robbed of wood to build the new palace, or were left to rot into the ground.

She shook her head against him. "I'm of an age with you, Aung, and you cannot tell me you would be ready for the labor needed to rebuild a whole city. No, I will be left behind, a beggar woman. I have been thinking of travelling to the south to become a nun. There are Christian communities there."

"That is foolish talk," he lied. "Bodawpaya will be king for many years."

With a sigh, she pulled away. "It is good that

you are a man who usually speaks the truth, for you are a terrible liar." She pulled her feet under her and stood, still as graceful as he remembered, or perhaps that part of his memory was also fading, but she looked down at him and offered her hand. "I think I must get back to work."

He clambered up beside her and they made their way back through the trees, talking of old times and the people they remembered and the way the sunset always gilded the many temple spires on the Sagaing Hills. Then he left her to follow the path back to the small house allotted to the visiting puppet troupe. The dust turned his damp feet blood red as he walked.

CHAPTER 3

Keeping to the shadows, Yamin ducked through the bushes and tall grass amid the trees. The old singer was truly easy to follow—anyone with half an ear could do it, for his footsteps shuffled across the dusty ground. His breath wheezed like a bellows, and his joints creaked like an old tree in the wind. Just how did these humans get so old, when, compared to him, they were so young?

He stayed close enough to hear what was said between the singer and the old woman. There was something between them. It was clear in the way their bodies curved toward each other like the necks of swans and yet they did none of the swooning and moaning that Minthamee did for the love of her Mintha. Something was different between these two. Perhaps it was that they were so—*old?*

Yet they dabbled their feet like children and probably the old man was not paying attention to all that the woman said because he was too lovey-dovey about the woman herself. Mintha and Minthamee were like that—so in love with each other that they never did anything for anybody else. So, for all his promises, clearly the singer was not going to find out who killed the Min. It was up to faithful Yamin to do something about it.

He waited until the singer started down the path toward the guesthouse and stepped out of the brush at the base of a flame tree.

"Well? Are you going to do it?" Yamin faced the singer with his hands on his hips. "Give us up and run off with that god of hers and her?"

The old singer staggered and clutched his chest. Then he checked around himself and bent down to Yamin. "What are you doing here? You shouldn't be out on your own."

His breath smelled fetid as old betel nut—the kind the singer chewed against aches and pains.

"Don't change the subject, old man." Yamin stamped his foot. "Are you leaving?"

The darn human was smiling! He held up his hands as if to fend off Yamin.

"I'm not going anywhere but back to the others, Yamin. The woman is an old and dear friend but I fear that, too, is ending, for her beliefs and mine are no longer in accord." His shoulders slumped as if a greater weight fell on them. Strange. He'd never had a conversation like this with a human. Mostly he poked fun at them and made them laugh. Just what do you say in a serious conversation?

"Oh. Well, then." Yamin toed the ground. "Did you solve the mystery? Did you learn who killed our Min?"

"Shh." The old man peered through the trees

as if his half-blind eyes might see better than Yamin's sharp ears could hear. "Not so loud. But it seems to me that if you heard her talk of changing faith then you likely learned as much as I did. So what did you think, Master Page? Who had reason to do us harm?"

For a moment Yamin could not believe what he'd heard. Then all his thoughts jammed up in his head so he felt like he might explode and leastwise everything he thought was probably not what the singer meant. He ground his fingernails into his palms and took a deep breath that couldn't quite quell everything he felt. "You want my thoughts? You want my help? I always wanted to solve a mystery, but no one ever lets me have any fun!"

Again the old man's lips curved as he nodded. "Tell me as we walk along." He started off and Yamin scampered to keep up.

"It seems to me that the list is endless."

The old singer looked down at him. "Really? You surprise me, Yamin, for your words echo my thoughts exactly."

He stopped on the path and Yamin puffed beside him. All the long years being carried in a basket didn't exactly make him fit to run all day—at least not anymore. Had he aged as well?

The old singer kindly picked him up and placed him on his left shoulder. "So tell me your list."

Yamin inhaled the old man's scent of betel and soapberry from his laundered paso and shirt. He held up his hand and began to tick his fingers off one by one. "Well the king, of course. He really sounds like he does not like you. It is something you might want to take up with him. Perhaps show him that you are really a good fellow, if quite old. But then he's old, too, isn't he? Perhaps you could become best of friends as you have so much in common."

The old singer held up his hand. "The list, Yamin. Who are our suspects?"

Yamin chewed his lip a moment sorting through what he'd overheard. "How about that vizier person? He doesn't want a war and worries that your song will push the king into making one. And what about the spies? If the foreign people are here they might want to weaken the king, though I can't quite figure how hurting us would do that." He scratched a persistent annoying itch at the base of one of his pony tails and grinned.

The old singer nodded. "Good thoughts, both of them. If we don't perform it would mean that the pwe performances are incomplete and therefore the marriage would not be approved by the nats. Even if nat worship is outlawed, that could weaken Bodawpaya in the eyes of those who still believe—the noble families and the people. But beyond spies, there may be someone closer to home who also would like to undermine a king."

The old man went silent and shivered under him, then: "Regicides are not uncommon. Bodawpaya came to power that way. Bagyidaw is old enough and itching for a crown of his own."

The crown prince? For a moment Yamin could not believe it, for it was impossible that Prince Mintha would ever raise a hand to the Min. Humans were so very different. "Would it not be dangerous for anyone in the royal enclosure during such a coup?"

"It would." The old singer bowed his head.

Yamin considered as he kicked his heels against the old man's boney chest, until the old singer set him down just before they arrived at the guesthouse.

"I thought of another one," Yamin grinned up at him, puffing his chest for this was very much like a guessing game and he was winning!

"Another?"

"Another suspect. How about the girl's lover? He wouldn't want the girl to marry. He'd have a reason to stop the spirit's blessing."

"Of course. Most insightful, Yamin. Now head off to your basket and keep to the bushes so that no one sees you."

Yamin grinned and started into the shadows and then stopped in his tracks. "I thought of another! It could be another puppet troupe. Or how about your friend? She doesn't sound like she likes the nats. Burning a spirit house, indeed!"

A troubled look filled the singer's gaze as if he did not want to hear such a possibility. He shook his head. "I think we have many more likely suspects. Now get back to the others."

Yamin rolled his eyes. So the human was being blind again. "Well, don't be surprised if you're wrong. How can you humans ever know just what another human is thinking?"

The singer waved him away. "And don't follow me again. It's too dangerous!"

Yamin turned on his heel and stuck out his tongue, then scooted into the shadows and brush before the old man could respond.

Chapter 4

Damnable sprite. Shaking his head at the effrontery of the brazen little page, Aung stepped around the last corner to the guest house.

U Winna and Saya Lin met Aung at the base of the ladder. Westward, the sky had turned blood red, and the shadows beneath the house had darkened. A cook fire had been started, lighting the space, and rice boiled and bubbled sending up a welcome scent that reminded Aung of how long it was since his last meal. The rest of the troupe looked on expectantly from shadows near the puppet trunks.

"So? Have you discovered our culprit?" U Winna and Saya Lin asked as one.

Aung shook his head as he fumbled his way up the ladder into the house, almost too tired to see. All the memories of his years with Daw Ma Sanda—of course in those days she had just been Sanda—had stirred emotions he had thought not still in his repertoire. And now he had lost her again, this time more permanently, to a suitor—this God—against whom he could not hope to compete. He could almost understand the king's desire for a young wife if she could help him recover those feelings of manhood that had been lost years before. As it was, a clot of sadness caught in his chest.

He collapsed onto an old man's stool by a bamboo mat and massaged his tired calves as U Winna and Saya Lin followed him up the ladder. "What of your enquiries?" he asked the two men. "Were there any people sighted near our guesthouse during last night's performance?"

"Nai Zaya heard that there were soldiers, but we have yet to find out who," said U Winna, assuming control of the situation. "U Myint heard that one of the queen's women was seen walking near here, but she may have simply been headed for the gate into the city. Otherwise, nothing."

Aung considered their words and what he knew. "We would need to learn who sent any soldiers. And as for the queen's woman, that may tell us nothing. And that leaves us exactly nowhere." Unless the queen's woman was the messenger sent by the queen-to-be... The doom of Min's death weighed upon him. Could it mean anything but death for them all? At the least it was a harbinger.

Saya Lin asked Thura to bring *lahpet* as a refreshment and settled himself on the bamboo carpet with U Winna.

Thura brought a tray with a meal of rice and small river fish, tea, and a lacquered partitioned bowl painted black with elaborate designs of the Great Nats—Min Mahagiri, Lady Three Times

Beautiful, the mighty Taungbyon Brothers, the white horse Nat, the rice mother, and others. The bowl's partitions held lahpet—pickled tea—in sesame oil in the center and condiments of dried shrimp, dried garlic, ground nuts and fried coconut in the compartments that spread like petals around the center. Thura bowed low before serving and then backed out of the room and down the ladder. Aung spooned up some of the tea, topped it with shrimp and fried coconut and closed his eyes at the pungent salty-sweet-tart concoction. He chewed and swallowed, then opened his eyes contentedly at the two other men. "Please have me put out of my misery on the day when I can no longer enjoy this treasure."

"Of all the fruit, the mango is best. Of all the meat, the pork is best, and of all the leaves, the lahpet's the best," Saya Lin intoned the old saw around a crunchy mouthful of tea and dried garlic. He sipped his green tea as he formed a rice ball around a sliver of fish.

U Winna chewed his mouthful, his hands resting on his belly's roundness as if it was a child he cared for.

"All this is good enough for a marriage feast," Aung said and lowered his voice so that it would not carry to the troupe. "It reminds me of where we are and why we are here. Rumors and half-truths abound in the palaces, but I am told that there are many surrounding this wedding. Did you know that Bodawpaya had already got wind of the songs I would sing?"

He considered each of the men, for perhaps one of them was responsible for that leak of information. For it to be another of the troupe would require them to studiously remember and join the snippets of words they might hear Aung sing, for Aung never sang the whole song together until the night of the pwe. Only U Winna and Saya Lin had heard all the words together. Both men looked away.

"I'm sorry old friend," U Winna said. "I shared the words. One of the king's officers came to me before we started upriver. He mentioned how hard things might be for Thiri in the palace if I did not cooperate and that he had connections who might ease her transition. To be one amongst the hundreds of the king's women—Thiri could be no more than a slave to the others." He sat there, shoulders slumped, like a man defeated. "I never foresaw this marriage. A good one, yes, for she had many suitors, but to the king… How is a simple man like me supposed to deal with such a thing?" He was suddenly a helpless father of the bride swept up by the tide of such events.

Aung sighed, his clue of the king knowing his song apparently all for naught. "I'm not sure it matters now. At first I thought perhaps the king himself had the troupe injured to stop the songs. But then I started to consider. The yoke thei are needed at the pwe to make the wedding auspicious for the nobles and common people. Why would he ruin such a thing if he truly wants this marriage?" He looked from man to man. "Can you think of a reason?"

U Winna grimaced. "Perhaps he has another puppet troupe available, one less likely to sing such songs?"

Saya Lin looked horrified. "If that was the case then the ruin of our Min would be just the excuse he would need to execute us for displeasuring him!"

"Think a moment," Aung said quietly. "If Bodawpaya truly wanted us dead, do you think he would hesitate to simply kill us? He has never required an excuse with anyone else. He could simply have left us in Arakan and called in this other troupe."

"Then who? Who would wish to destroy us?" Saya Lin asked.

Aung left off mention of the girl's possible lover and told them of the rumors of the vizier's concerns, foreign spies, and possibly the prince's scheming as the last red streaks bled westward from the sky. Beyond the open face of the guesthouse the royal enclosure turned shadowed so that every bush was filled with spies.

Aung shook his head. "So I ask myself who would profit if this marriage does not go forward or if it does go forward without the nats' favor. Let us remember that the country has already been riled by the king's proclamation that the Alchemists are heretics who must be destroyed and that the nats must not be worshipped. If he further affronts the Great Nats and the nats of the land by not having the traditional performance to propitiate them, in some people's eyes he may be unfit to rule. People may believe that he is the reason the rains do not come. That might give others the reason to replace him."

"But surely even Bodawpaya would not go forward with the wedding without the traditional blessing of the nats?" U Winna asked.

The sound of the troupe's quiet voices as they finished their meal came from beneath them and then a clear true voice rose in a quiet song—Thura—singing the bedtime song that tamed the unruliness of the yoke thei, for they were a temperamental lot who could give their puppeteers many problems. It was only the magical silver strings coiled in the little ones' raven hair that allowed the puppeteers and their puppets to provide the seamless performances the troupe was known for. The silver strings allowed yoke thei and puppeteer to become as one.

"Would that the Nats would tell us what they know, for are they not privy to all the world's secrets?" Saya Lin said, as he studied his hands. The appetite for the laphet seemed to have fled the Master puppeteer, too. Only U Winna still nibbled at spoons-full from the bowl.

"If only we could ask them," Aung said and felt fatigue roll through him. His back ached. His shoulders, too, and the thought of his bed was a comfort to him. But the troupe needed him. Their lives depended upon it.

"Of course!" He straightened and slapped his knee. "The Min! Surely he would know who killed him! We can ask the yoke thei. They can still commune with their brethren because they are of the same tree spirit!"

Saya Lin scrambled up and helped Aung to his feet.

U Winna looked up at them. "What are you talking about? Min is dead."

"The puppets share the tree's spirit and can commune with each other through more than wood—perhaps even when one of their number is in the cloud fields of the north. We must ask them!" Saya Lin said and helped Aung down the stairs.

Under the house the puppets were being readied for slumber while the musicians cleaned up the remains of the meal. The Ministers preened as their cloaks were straightened. The white horse folded his legs under him and laid his head down on his silken bed. A puff of incense filled the area under the house as the little horse returned to his wood. The handmaid followed the horse and the naga dragon. The Alchemist set down his wand and the Votaress laid her head on her pillow. The little Minthamee complained that her puppeteer pulled her hair too hard as he brushed out the luxurious length.

Yamin tumbled and cartwheeled around the

area under the house staying just out of reach of his puppeteer's grasp. "I don't want to go to bed," he cried. "I want to solve the mystery instead!" Where did the little one get so much energy?

"Wait," Aung said. "To solve this mystery I have a request. Someone must travel to the cloud fields of the north and ask the Min who destroyed his wood."

"Well I, for one, am willing to go." Yamin stopped his tumbling in front of Aung, his hands on his hips, his chest puffed out like a mating bird.

Aung sighed. He should have thought this through. After his meeting with the little page earlier he should have known this would happen. He glanced at Saya Lin. "Is Yamin the best one for the task?"

"Of course I'm the best one for the task. I'm quick and funny and I want to go!" he stamped his small bare foot. "I'm *interested*!"

Aung bent down to him. "But Yamin, are there not others that the Min might be more willing to speak with? Perhaps the lovely Minthamee, or one of his Ministers?"

"You'll not send Minthamee anywhere without me," said the Mintha, leaping from the top of his basket to Minthamee's side. "She is a princess, not to be sent like a messenger on a singer's work."

Aung bowed. "Then perhaps yourself, my Prince?"

"But I want to go!" Yamin tugged insistently at

the hem of Aung's paso.

Mintha half bowed. "If it is important, I will do as you ask." He returned to his basket and lay down. Incense perfumed the air and his spirit was gone. Only wood remained.

A small heel smashed into Aung's toe. Yamin glared up at him. "I could have done it, too, if you'd let me." He stomped off to his wicker basket and threw himself down. A puff of incense and the space under the house became suddenly quiet and less filled with energy.

"For such a little one, he takes up a fair amount of room," Aung said rubbing his injured toe on the back of his other leg.

Saya Lin nodded.

"We will let the Mintha commune and then speak with him in the morning. I suggest we set a guard and the others get a good night's sleep. Who knows what tomorrow will bring," Aung said.

Amidst disheartened murmurs Aung, U Winna, and Saya Lin left the troupe and climbed the ladder into the guest house. Too tired for discussion, too tired for thought, Aung threw himself down on a bamboo mat and was instantly asleep.

CHAPTER 5

In the cloud fields of the north the air was sweet and cold and filled with white mist. Far below lay the jutting peaks of what were surely the highest mountains in the world. Snow fell there, and melted. Rivers ran and tore the sides of the mountains down. Birds flew through the mountain passes and humans and animals struggled to eke out an existence. All which mattered not a whit to Yamin.

He worked the shoulders of his spirit body—spectral thin and light enough air ran through his bones, and his broad translucent gossamer wings caught the currents of air that took him up to the clouds. Somewhere ahead the Mintha flew, and he was strong and powerful, but he did not care about this mission as much as Yamin did. Surely wanting to do this thing would make Yamin fly faster!

He swooped and soared, searching the currents of air for the fastest. Catching one, he stretched out his arms and dove. Wind rushed through his ears. Wind caught in his wings and almost tore the fragile membrane, but that was the price you must pay if you want to do something important!

There. Ahead the clouds thickened around a mighty peak and the air filled with the sound of small bells and singing. Yoke thei spirits. Many of them danced in rainbows amidst the starlight.

Yamin tumbled down among them. "The Min who is alone—where is he? I must speak to him."

The yoke thei tumbled and laughed around him as if he was their entertainment.

"I mean it! I'm serious! I need to find him!" By all the naga in the sea, why did no one believe him? These were his people. They should know him.

Finally a handmaid took pity on him. "There is no Min who is alone, but there is one who has a Mintha with him." She pointed to an eddy in the crystalline air where two winged beings hung close together.

Yamin thanked her and swooped through the air. "I'm here. I'm here. I want to know!"

"What are you doing here?" the Mintha said. In his yoke thei spirit form he was still larger than Yamin, with wings that would span the hands of two large human men. "The old human asked *me* to speak to Min." He flapped his wings, and the resulting wind sent Yamin tumbling.

Yamin righted himself and, mumbling at stupid princes who thought they were something, he hurried back in time to hear the Mintha ask the king who had killed him.

The Min was larger than Mintha, with wide golden wings and broad shoulders and a proud bearing to his golden head. His flowing hair caught the wind. Everyone always walked carefully around the Min, for like his human counterpart he was quick to anger and apparently had a dearth of humor. But he put up with antics of his page—at least so far.

Min shook his head impatiently. "How should I know? I was slumbering and enjoying the cloud fields amongst my brethren." He motioned wide with his arms at the laughing spirits and the spun silver clouds. "I felt my body move and then the pain. Then it was over. My perfect body was no more." His lips thinned and his gaze flashed. "It was a despicable act. The culprit must be caught and I will personally see that he dies on the stake!" His voice vibrated with anger.

The Mintha bowed so his head was level with Min's feet. He backed away as if he was done.

Yamin swooped in. "But you can't stop there. There's more we need to know! Your Majesty, great Min, I apologize for disturbing you, but what else did you sense?"

Mintha caught his arm and dragged him away. "I'm sorry Your Majesty. He is a troublesome boy who shall be punished in his body."

Yamin jerked away and rushed back to the king. "I'm not just a small boy! I'm old as him! And you! Did you hear anyone? Smell anyone? Was anything different? Think back to the time before the event."

Min went thoughtful and Yamin glared over

his shoulder at Mintha.

Finally Min shook his head. "I appreciate your efforts little one, but there is nothing for me to remember. Everything was as it always was. There were no strange smells or sounds for me to hear."

Yamin sighed. He'd had such hope. Perhaps he was just as bad an investigator as Mintha seemed to think. "Truly? There was nothing? No different feel in the air around you?"

Min showed an inordinate amount of patience, then he shook his head again. "Nothing. It all happened so fast. But I seem to recall hands holding me tight. And anger. A great deal of anger. That is all I can say." He bowed his head and clearly the audience was over.

Yamin carefully bowed and backed away, then turned to Mintha. He stuck out his tongue. "Race you!"

He dove through the sky and let the wind lift him.

~~~

Aung bolted upright at the sound of commotion below the house floor.

"You are nothing but trouble! You think you are funny, but you are not! You are tiresome and unwanted! Do you hear? Unwanted!"

"I was just trying to help," Yamin's carrying voice soared through the darkness. "And I am so funny! People laugh!"

"What is it? What's going on?" U Winna
~~~

mumbled still caught in slumber.

All was still darkness though the night sky showed the faintest hope of fading. Aung fumbled to his feet. "I think the communing is finished. The Mintha has woken. And Yamin, too, by the sound."

He clambered down the ladder, his joints groaning worse than the wood. Underneath the house all was darkness except for a small pool of firelight where U Thant, the dragon drummer, had stirred last night's cook fire to life. Puppeteers were rubbing their eyes—all except two who were trying to separate their two bristling charges. Mintha and Yamin faced each other, both flushed with anger. The Mintha had drawn himself into a regal pose. Yamin's little body positively vibrated and his pony tails shook.

"Well, you are not a help. Never a help. Why didn't you just go to your bed and leave the Min to your betters?" Mintha said.

Other wicker baskets began to vibrate as all the noise woke the other yoke thei. Puppeteers hurried to sooth them, because unrested puppets could mean ill-tempers all day.

"Well maybe it's because I, myself, want to solve a mystery, not simply look good to Minthamee." The little page jutted his chin as he glared up at the taller prince.

Wicker baskets tops burst open and puppets sat up.

"Now, now, my two fine fellows. I take it that you both went to speak to Min. I thank you. Pray what information did the king provide?" Aung looked from one to the other and gentled them apart.

"See?" Yamin said. "*He* knows I'm worth something. I'm helping him investigate." He crossed his arms over his vest.

Mintha looked from Aung to the page. "A lie surely."

"Tell him, Master Aung. Tell him I'm not lying!"

The voices of the other puppets rose as Aung looked from the burly, somewhat arrogant prince to the troublesome little page. The little one looked so beseeching that he could not find the words to put Yamin in his place. "Yamin has shown some good insights." He nodded.

"There! You see?" Yamin stuck out his tongue at the prince.

"Yamin! That is not polite or appropriate," his puppeteer said.

"Come. Tell me what you've learned." Aung settled himself uncomfortably on the ground by the sputtering fire.

Mintha shook his head. "I asked, but there is nothing to tell. Min did not see his killer. He didn't even have time to rouse from his wood when the blow was struck that sent him to the cloud fields forever."

Yamin rolled his eyes. "That's all he asked him: 'Do you know who killed you? Of course he didn't know. But I asked him other questions, like whether he remembered anything else, any sounds or sights or smells."

"You badgered him until he sent us away!" Mintha cried. He turned to Aung. "He was a pest. A pestilence, I tell you."

"You have done your duty. It is well done. Now let us get you back to your basket, my prince," his puppeteer, soothed.

Aung thanked him for his efforts and let the muttering prince stalk away. Aung turned a disapproving look at Yamin. "You did not have to rile him so, little one."

"He's bossy and he thinks he's so important because he's the prince, but I get to sing your songs, Master Aung. The special songs that you make for the king. I *know* I'm important."

And he was full of himself because of it, but he was as eager to please as a puppy.

"So what did you learn from all your questions?"

Yamin danced a little two step and then plopped cross-legged in front of him. His puppeteer shook his head with a rueful grin as if to say Aung did not know what he'd got himself into.

Yamin leaned in close and, wonder of wonders, lowered his voice. "Mintha is right in that much: Min did not see who killed him. But he did not smell anything or hear anything unusual either. All he felt was the killer's hands—and anger. It is as if the killer just suddenly appeared and did his damage and disappeared again. Very strange, I for one am thinking. It's like no one was there who should not have been."

"Well that clearly is not the case, is it? All of us are too dependent on the health of our puppets," Aung sighed. Clearly his work was cut out for him and he was not sure exactly where to look next. Every clue seemed to lead to a dead end.

A puppeteer's cry cut through his thoughts. "He is not here. He is not anywhere!" U Myint pushed past other puppeteers, shoving yoke thei aside to peer into their baskets.

"Who is not here?" Aung demanded, struggling back to his feet.

"Garuda!" U Myint went from basket to basket, knocking them over in his frantic search. Garuda was the great half man-half bird who carried the god Vishnu into battle. Garuda was the greatest warrior, at one time defeating even the gods. U Myint returned to one particular basket at the edge of the covered area. "He was right here. I know it, but his basket is empty!"

The guesthouse was in uproar.

"Silence!" Aung commanded using his stage voice.

Everyone obeyed.

"U Myint. You will search for Garuda in the trees around the guesthouse. Perhaps he simply wished to stretch his wings. Thura, go with him and help—don't just get underfoot." But a sickness in his belly told Aung that this was more than just a Garuda flexing his wings. He glanced up at Saya

Lin and shook his head. Saya Lin paled.

"So who do we talk to next, Master Aung? What do we do next to catch our killer?" Little Yamin still waited at his feet.

Aung sighed again as U Myint's voice drifted back from the bushes. "What indeed. I will need to think on this awhile." He looked up at the others. "Everyone to bed. But first bring the yoke thei baskets farther under the house. We will post a guard and sleep around them this night and as long as we remain in the king's enclosure."

He looked down at Yamin who looked up at him. "Go to your basket Master Page and pray, no more adventures on your own."

Yamin frowned as if that was exactly what he'd planned. Finally he nodded, hopped up and scampered to his basket.

"Have a care with him. I found him out in the gardens today," Aung said to Yamin's puppeteer.

Aung returned to the guesthouse, but sleep was beyond him. Instead, he sat cross-legged and meditated on their problem as the sky eastward gradually blushed the color of a young girl's cheeks, and the sun laced the heavens with columns of light.

The garuda, now. The mount of celestial kings. Was there meaning in the choice of puppet? That the king cannot escape? Or was it simply to instill fear and hopelessness in the puppeteers? How could they perform like this? Should they run while they still could?

Color crept into the king's gardens, first hinting at green leaves, then the bright reds and yellows of the calla lilies. The birds woke and twittered and sang. The peacock squawked and spread his tail feathers. From beyond the enclosure walls came the sounds of Amarapura's awakening, but in the gardens it was as quiet as in the great forests of the world.

In the forests the health of the trees and animals was ruled over by the *taw saun*—the forest protector nat who begrudgingly allowed humans to take from his bounty. If he was not propitiated, though, it could be disaster for the human involved. Once this enclosure had been forest, too.

Aung straightened. Did the taw saun still rule here even though the king had reduced the forest to no more than a garden? If so perhaps the forest nat could tell him something. They were old, wise creatures who knew everything that went on in their domain.

That would be his next step. There had to be a *nat kadaw*, a shrine, somewhere in the royal enclosure, for though Bodawpaya had little use for the spirits of the land, Aung could not imagine that all the people of the enclosure had turned away from the old ways. Surely at such a shrine he could call on the taw saun to reveal the secrets of the royal enclosure, for such creatures were steeped in secrets and whispers.

He stood and started down the ladder as Saya Lin stirred and stretched. "Where are you going?"

Aung held his finger to his lips. "Better I don't say for there are little ears below," he whispered. From in the gardens he still heard U Myint softly calling, but it was doubtful that there would ever be an answer.

Aung climbed down and crept away from the guest house, praying that Yamin hadn't seen him go. Yes, the little page might have good insights, but he was also trouble—too brash, too impetuous, and too quick to temper. He had no subtlety to him at all, and dealing with a taw saun would certainly require that. With the troupe's lives in the balance he could not afford to have the nats against them, too.

Chapter 6

In the dimly lit morning, Aung set out through the gardens as quickly as his old man's legs could carry him. He needed answers swiftly, and the garden path would be slower, but his path would be less remarked. A nat kadaw would most likely be at the edge of the royal enclosure, somewhere along the inside of the wall; his best bet was that it would be at one of the corners. Unfortunately, that meant that unless he was lucky, he could find himself having to walk a very long way today. At his pace it would take a long time, too—time they did not have to solve this mystery. He sighed. And he had not had breakfast. He tightened his paso around his waist. He would manage somehow if he could just make his search go faster.

He reached the tall, white wall of the enclosure with dawn's obscuring mist still spread through the trees. The air was still cool. He turned west toward the river and strode as quickly as his old legs would allow. The Ayarewaddy's scent was rich and murky, as if its low water had exposed something bad. Along the walls night blooming flowers closed their secret hearts against the day.

By the gates, soldiers stopped him. "What

brings you out so early, old man?" The soldier was young and clearly a Bayingyi, a part blood Portuguese by his pale eyes and long nose. Suspicion filled his gaze, so clearly the soldiers were ill at ease, too. The entire enclosure reeked with danger.

"I am with the puppeteers. I—I go for a walk to stretch these old legs." He held up his hands, weaponless, but the soldier frisked him anyway.

The soldier frowned. "Get on with you, then. Don't come near the gates again unless you mean to leave."

Aung hurried away. Perhaps he and the troupe should simply escape. Of course, Bodawpaya's wrath would likely have them hunted down and killed, but at least for a few more days they would be free, not trapped in a place of secrets, spies and subterfuge.

Perhaps the danger was what had set him on this investigation most of all. After so many years of performing, this meant *more*. He could feel his heart pumping, old muscles working in his legs and his brain working harder than it had in years. He felt almost young again. Like a young warrior protecting his family instead of an old man falling into infirmity and dotage. He had to succeed!

He reached the first corner having found no sign of a nat kadaw and turned south as the sun grew higher and leaned on his shoulders. His stomach protested, but he kept going, looking ahead to the compound's distant next corner.

There was nothing on the eastern side of the enclosure except the entry gates. He followed the walls eastward, coming to the broad gates that led to the royal harbor and barges in the shallows of the royal lake. There were more guards here.

"Old man!" One of the guards blocked Aung's way.

~~~

It was so unfair! Yamin pushed through the trees. Even the old singer had betrayed him, going to investigate without him. He clenched his fists and kicked at a leaf.

Didn't they understand that just because he was small didn't mean that he had no head on his shoulders? He'd *thought* the old man might actually have some sense and have figured that out. Instead, when Yamin had woken, he'd found the old man had gone—and no one knew where!

"Drat him! Drat him! Drat!" Another leaf felt his attack. "Old man, you almost make me think you don't want my help."

He stopped, the afternoon sun filtering through the leaves above him. Of *course* the old singer wanted his help—he was just old and had *forgotten* to wake Yamin or leave word of where he went.

"So just where would you go if you were a singer investigating the death of a Min?" He tapped his finger aside of his nose as he considered.
~~~

It surely wasn't an easy problem, because in all his years Yamin had never made a study of humans. They were just overly large and clumsy beings who happened to have a say in the yoke thei performances.

He sat on his heels to rest for this royal compound surely was a big place. Almost as big as the world, it seemed. The old singer seemed bent on gathering information and he needed to be quick about it, given the disappearance of garuda. My goodness, the disappearance of the bird could mean that all the yoke thei were in danger. Even him.

He eyed the suddenly less-than-friendly bushes around him, a little less happy about being about on his own. "If anything happens to me, it shall be your fault, old man!"

But the forest had always been the friend of the yoke thei. After all, being bits of trees, were they not kin to the taw saun? Now there was a being who knew everything that went on in its forest—from the fall of the smallest sparrow to the newly woken seed of the Yamani as it took root. Perhaps the taw saun could tell him where the old man had gone.

Or perhaps the forest spirit could tell him who killed the Min! He could show up the old Singer and everyone!

He sprang to his feet and closed his eyes, breathing deep of the air under the trees. It was just a little sweeter to the east. The taw saun had to be there.

He set out at a jog as the sun rose its highest and began to sink westward. He kept to shadows between the palaces and avoided the royal gardeners and the palace dogs. And cats. There were some larger than he was that he barely managed to scare off by leaping at them from a tree branch.

The sweetness in the air grew stronger, the trees thicker and more lush, even in the time of drought. He slowed and felt the forest's regard around him and the trees' breath. He went to his knees.

"I'm here, mighty taw saun," he said and bowed his head to the ground, for the forest spirits were as quick to anger as all the nats and they could do terrible things when their ire was raised.

A slight breeze rippled through the forest and Yamin knew he was no longer alone. He peeked upwards and found the taw saun regarding him.

The guardian of the forest was a comely being, as tall as a human but with garlands of green moss for hair and skin as dark and cracked as tree bark. His face was handsome by human standards, though his eyes carried the green glow of tree sap and sunlight on leaves. His mouth turned down, though, as if he wasn't exactly happy to see a yoke thei.

"Little brother," the taw saun said. "Why are you here—alone? Where are your tree brethren?"

Yamin scrambled to his feet and drew himself

up to his most serious personage. "Actually, they are waiting at the king's guesthouse. But there is a problem. Someone has killed the Min and everything is close to ruin. I'm investigating the killing. I thought perhaps you might have information that can help me."

The taw saun's green brow arched his doubt and for a moment Yamin was afraid. He could lie and cajole his way around humans and even the other yoke thei, but perhaps it was not a good idea doing it here.

"I am too, investigating. I'm helping the old singer." By all the naga in the ocean, why did no one believe him? The only one who had listened to him at all was the old singer and perhaps that was half-heartedly. He sighed. "I have been helping, but today he left me behind. I thought I, myself, could help him by coming to see you."

The truth hung between them until the taw saun stirred and looked beyond Yamin to the forest.

"So where is Aung Aung, then? I have watched him sing for many years. He is a great man and a friend to spirits."

"You have? He is?" In all the years Yamin had travelled with the troupe, he'd never truly noticed. Just another human, although he had sung some of the most clever songs of all. Songs that even set Yamin giggling.

The taw saun swung around to regard the forest. "He is there. Bring him to me if you would.

Bring him to the shrine. I think we have words to share."

The taw saun stepped back towards the trees, his form fading into the shadows under the leaves. Yamin exhaled when he hadn't even realized he was holding his breath.

Dealing with spirits was never easy.

~~~

Finally free of the soldiers at the lake gate to the royal enclosure, Aung hurried along the eastern wall. Fatigue made him faint and his belly ached with hunger, but it was troubling thoughts that consumed him. The soldier at the gate had implied that some great personage was coming. To attend the pwe? The marriage ceremony? Could it be related to what had happened? Did the important personage not want the marriage to occur? Or was it someone who wanted to undermine the king? Either way his list of suspects just kept growing. He groaned as he walked through the shade of the trees. Here, on the eastern side of the enclosure, the trees were thicker, the underbrush less tamed. The bird song increased.

"You make noise like that and everyone will think you are dying." Yamin stepped out from between the tall grass at the base of a frangipani tree. He tapped his toes and looking Aung up and down. "You look like you could fall down. You aren't taking very good care of that body of yours. You know it's one of the things that I, myself, have
~~~

always wondered about with humans. Why do you not care for yourselves better so that you don't grow so *old?*"

Aung stopped dead, uncertain what to say. He looked down at the little page. "I thought you promised to stay home in your basket."

"I did no such thing! People might have *told* me to stay in my basket." He looked meaningfully at Aung out of the tops of his eyes. "That doesn't mean I *promised*. Besides, you needed my help. You're looking for the taw saun, aren't you? That's what you've been doing all morning. Well, while you've been wandering around, I've found him for you. He says he will talk to you if you come to him." He waited, peering up at Aung who looked into the shadowed forest.

"I did good, didn't I?" He almost doubted himself at Aung's silence.

"Yes. Yes, you did well, though I would have eventually found the taw saun myself."

"I doubt it. His shrine isn't along the walls where you were looking. According to the tree voices, the king had that nat kadaw torn down last year. The new one is hidden in the trees." He beckoned Aung to follow and, with nary a rustle, disappeared back into the long grass at the base of the trees. Aung hurried to follow lest he lose his small guide.

He needn't have worried. Yamin kept up a constant chatter about his suspicions. The vizier plotting. The prince as well. And spies. He hid behind bushes and practiced peering out. "That's what spies do, isn't it? Sneak around?"

"Yes, Yamin." The little puppet's boundless energy just emphasized Aung's growing exhaustion and the way pain cramped his steps. He really had underestimated the distance he would have to walk. Once upon a time he could have run it in an hour. Sometimes he forgot that time and age were the eternal enemies—but not for little puppets made of wood, apparently. Around them the tamed gardens had given way to an untamed corner of wildwood with taller trees and thickening brush between them so the sunlight cast only dim shadows through the canopy of leaves. As if by magic, the air turned cooler and was sweetened by small golden flowers that starred the shadows under the trees.

"Here we are!" Yamin crowed and was gone, scampering through a last screen of trees.

Cautiously, Aung shoved aside the brush and slipped into a clearing surrounded by walls of thick bush and tree trunks. Aung expected bright sunlight and the heat of the day, but overhead the tree's spreading branches masked the sky and cast shifting green shadows over the grass and scattered white and purple wild flowers. Bees hummed and the air felt heavy like lightning, but beyond the tree branches Aung glimpsed unmarred blue.

In the center of the clearing stood a carved teak nat kadaw. Formed like a miniature palace placed on a four-foot pole, its steep lintels were ornately carved like naga dragons, its sides like scales. Inside the house stood a small carved figure of the handsome taw saun, clad in green cloth, with a green turban tied around his dark brow.

Around the base of the house were the fading remains of offerings: banana leaf platters with rice and fruit left behind. Stubs of incense sticks. A strip of golden cloth.

Yamin scampered off, chasing a butterfly and Aung bowed low to the nat kadaw, his palms pressed together by his forehead in respect. The air throbbed around him.

"Mighty taw saun, I beg your aid in solving the crime that has ruined one of your spirit brethren, the Min of the yoke thei. I fear the same fate has taken a second of the small ones."

To rest while he waited, he settled awkwardly on the ground. Whispers rustled in the shimmering green leaves. Bird voices faded far away and a growing green-gold glimmer filled the corners of his vision. Hunger surely, though his stomach had finally given up its rumbling even at the sight of the food offerings. Cool air like a monsoon breeze caressed his skin and he woke with a start when his chin hit his chest. How long had he slept? Had the taw saun come and gone? Had he missed his chance? The air vibrated around him like the tremor after heat lightning bringing his meager defenses to high alert.

"Here he is! See! I told you he wanted to talk

to you!" Yamin's cheerful chattering broke the anxious spell.

Aung blinked and rubbed his eyes at the strange man-creature who materialized from the trees.

Shaped like a man with two arms and two legs, the nat's glossy brown flesh was filled with bark-like cracks. Shaggy moss covered his pate, but it was his eyes that held Aung immobile. Green-gold and old—beyond the trees and rivers, beyond the hills and the deepest caves to when the first growing thing seeded. The green gold simmered with anger as he peered down at Aung.

"Singer. I have heard your songs for many years." The nat's sonorous voice sent a tremor through the trees and Aung's heart beat faster, for a nat was just as likely to destroy those who asked for aid as to help them.

"Your words are remembered under the eaves of the trees even though you must be very old." The deep voice softened and for a moment the eyes were just the soft green of leaves. "You make me laugh at the foolishness of kings." His voice had turned as musical as a spring breeze, but there was an undercurrent of anger.

"That—that is high praise, indeed." Aung bowed his head, uncertain whether to kowtow with his head touching the earth for surely this one would destroy him. "I would stand, but I fear these old legs of mine will refuse and I would collapse at your feet. Thank you for meeting me."

The taw saun glanced at Yamin. "Your young helper has told me of your mystery and that you seek my aid."

"I told him that I was helping with the investigation!" Yamin added. There was a plea in his eyes for Aung to agree.

He nodded slowly. "He has had some useful insights."

The little page grinned and did an unseemly cartwheel across the clearing, but such were the mercurial moods of Yamin.

The taw saun watched the page as if he could not quite believe Aung's words. Then he closed his eyes and for a moment it was as if the clearing wavered so that the darkness and danger of the day reached for Aung. Then the taw saun opened his eyes and the glowing clearing returned. Aung shivered and glanced at Yamin. Just how long had the page been visiting?

"I came out here this morning, Master Aung," Yamin said as if reading his mind.

Had Aung spoken his question out loud? He felt confused and uncertain.

Yamin stuck out his chin as if daring a reprimand.

Aung just shook his head. "Your puppeteer will be very worried. You will frighten the troupe. They will think you have disappeared like garuda."

Yamin's chin lowered, his stiff-necked defiance melting until he looked like a chastened child. "I'm sorry." His toe trailed in the soil.

Aung rolled his eyes. "No, you aren't sorry, are you, you little scamp!"

Yamin turned a soulfully pained gaze on him. And then grinned, all his even white teeth exposed.

Aung looked up at the taw saun. "Forgive us, please. I fear he may have been difficult if he was with you all morning."

An affectionate smile grazed the nat's lips as he glanced down at Yamin, who had thrown himself on the ground to study a crawling caterpillar. "It was not so long in the life of a tree. He makes me feel young again, when the world was full of wonder."

Aung just felt old. "Have you information that will help me?"

The taw saun closed his eyes again and the clearing wavered one more time. Darkness flooded around the tree trunks until he opened his eyes. "The trees are full of rumors. Wars to come or be stopped. An old king. A young prince. The end of a dynasty. A marriage to be stopped. Songs to be sung—or not—and anger. So much anger that it frightens the clouds so they do not come north to deliver their rain. The tree-roots wither and there is nothing I can do about it."

The tree shadows spread across the clearing and the taw saun faded and grew until there was only darkness, the sound of wind-torn leaves, and his huge furious gaze burning in the air.

Aung cringed back and fought for words. "But among all those rumors, who would want to kill the Min or take the garuda? It stops our performance and dooms us all. Have we enemies within the palace?"

The taw saun closed his eyes again but this time the unnatural darkness parted. He was a human-sized being with a wild tangle of moss on his head. The day passed away in a glory of golden leaves and true dusk descended. Through the tree branches overhead Aung caught a glimpse of stars. How long had he been here? Had he stepped beyond the confines of the world? Then he felt the taw saun's regard like cool leaves on his face.

"Not enemies. It is just that their desires run different than yours. There is no malice towards your puppeteers."

"Was it the song that I planned to sing? Has the king turned against us?"

The taw saun looked distracted. He circumnavigated the nat kadaw, running his fingers along the fine edges of the leaves so they flashed golden. "Though your words have long annoyed the king and amused the nats, I do not think it is the king. But someone—a leader of men—wishes to undermine the wedding. That is all that I know."

The green-gold of the taw sawn's gaze grew, and Aung found himself falling into their well. Shadows shifted in their depth as if the nat would show him something, but what it was, he couldn't tell. Swirls of gold and green filled his head and froze his thoughts like a drink of truly cold water.

He swayed where he sat, but the day's efforts had their affect.

He fell.

The green grass cushioned his cheek. The last thing he felt was the taw saun's cool touch on his brow.

"Sleep safely, old friend. There are dangers all around you, for the Great Nats do not countenance the death of the Min."

The night went black.

Chapter 7

Aung woke to birdsong so poignant and new for a moment he thought he was new born again. He struggled up to sitting, the ground covered with the first dew of the evening. Before him the nat kadaw was a specter of jagged ridges and angles, the odor of the old offerings gone rotten and he felt sick to his stomach. There was no sign of the taw saun.

The taw saun's words echoed in his head and hopelessness descended. If the Great Nats were also angry, they would not help him. And just how was an old man to bring a leader of men to justice? He thought of the nobles and royals and their invisible cloaks of power that he could never hope to equal.

"So you are finally awake. For a while, there, I thought you might have died but then you started snoring." The irreverent voice could only be Yamin, but fading vision and darkness hid the little page.

"Come here, you scamp. You kept watch over me, didn't you?" What he'd thought were two barely visible tassels of long grass became Yamin's two jaunty pony tails as the little page obeyed.

"I thank you, Yamin. You have turned out to be a most able assistant in this investigation. I'll not doubt you again."

"Well, it is about time." Yamin plopped down, cross-legged, in front of him again. "So what do we do now, Master Singer? Go back to the others? Continue our investigation?"

Aung studied his hands in the dim light. The knuckles were large and boney, and they shook just the slightest amount. Not the strong hands that would be needed to bring a leader of men to justice. "I am flummoxed, Yamin. How are we to detect who wants to undermine the wedding? To sneak around the royal enclosure to find the culprit… I fear it is beyond me and these old bones."

"But not beyond me!" Yamin leapt up with his usual over-exuberance. "I could skulk about like a spy and find our culprit."

Aung shook his head. "I don't think that's a good idea. We cannot risk you. If you were seen or caught it would be a disaster for the troupe and for you. In this age when the king has outlawed the worship of the nats you could be destroyed just as Min was. It's too dangerous for a small boy."

Yamin's shoulders sagged, but he nodded. "I, myself, think you are wrong, but I was afraid you would say that."

Aung struggled to his feet. "We should get back to the others. They will be worried. We've been gone too long."

As if sensing Aung's weakness, Yamin stayed close by his side, pointing out sticks across their path so that Aung didn't stumble. It was a kind side of Yamin he'd not seen before, and he found himself reaching down to catch the little one's hand for balance. While his footfall was uneven and sent twigs and branches crackling, Yamin was silent as the breeze around them.

It was moonrise by the time they reached the guesthouse. In the hot night an unnecessary fire blazed from under the house like an eye through the darkness. Aung stumbled into the circle of light where the entire troupe sat in desolation. They leapt to their feet when they saw Aung.

"Where have you been?" U Winna demanded.

"We thought you'd been arrested. Both of you! What do you have to say for yourselves?" Saya Lin's anger sent Yamin hiding behind Aung's paso.

Aung waved the questions away and sank to a stool Thura hurriedly brought him. When he'd caught his breath he scanned the faces surrounding him. "We—Yamin and I—have been conducting the investigation. We spoke to the taw saun."

Yamin stepped in front of him his fists raised. "Maybe you should bring him food before you question him. He hasn't eaten all day. He's very weak."

The puppeteers looked at each other as if they could not believe what they heard coming from Yamin's mouth. The page was not known for his concern for others. Then Thura rushed to bring a bowl of rice and fish that he'd set aside. Aung scooped the luscious meal up with his fingers and smacked his lips at the nutty flavor. He offered small bits to Yamin, who graciously accepted.

"So?" U Winna asked when Aung was partway through the meal. "What did you learn from the taw saun that was worth worrying the rest of us to death? The performance is days away. We need to solve this or escape."

Aung sighed, feeling as old as the Sagaing Hills, but without the glory of their many temples. "He said the culprit is a leader of men. Someone with a reason to stop the wedding. That seems to narrow our enquiry down to the nobles and great councilors. What news of garuda?"

"Only this." Saya Lin held out a single green-gold feather. "They found it in the forest."

Yamin tugged on Aung's sleeve.

"Yes, my friend?"

"Didn't your friend yesterday say that there were rumors that the new queen had already taken a lover? Maybe it's him."

"The new queen?!" U Winna bristled, his face flushed. "Never! My Thiri would never dishonor her family."

"Not even if her suitor was a prince?" Yamin asked.

Bagyidaw? Could it really be so? Yes, there were lesser princes, but if it was Bagyidaw it would explain so much.

"Never. Thiri is a good girl. My favorite, with her sweet face and voice."

"Such a sweet voice and face attracted a king. Why not a prince?" Aung asked softly. "I think I must sleep on these ideas and decide what to do in the morning." With Thura's help he stood.

"Good night my faithful helper," he bowed to Yamin. He nodded to the others and started up the ladder to his mat.

U Winna grabbed his arm. "I'll not have you ruining my daughter's reputation. Do you understand?"

It took everything Aung had to nod. He left the fuming master for the quiet of the guesthouse. U Winna's angry mutterings followed him into his slumber.

He woke in the night to the feeling that he had missed something, he just couldn't say what. He rose as silently as his age would allow and stepped over U Winna and Saya Lin for the ladder. Even in slumber, in the dim light of the moon, U Winna scowled as if his recent unhappiness bloomed just as large in his dreams. Saya Lin lay curled away with his back to the door. Trusting, that was always the way with Saya Lin—until you proved yourself unworthy. Then you ceased to exist for the Master Puppeteer. It was a matter of pride that Aung had been friends with the other man for nigh on forty years.

He eased himself down the ladder and away from the shadows underneath, praying that Yamin would remain asleep. Then he retraced his steps to the vizier's kitchens. At this time of the night all was in darkness, the kitchen fires banked to embers. The moon shadows twisted the building's graceful, carved lintels into contorted shapes that could be nagas coiled to strike with many hooded heads, just as someone's heart had been contorted to do what they had to the Min. He set himself in the shadows to wait, certain that the one he wanted would eventually appear.

The night sky was clear and filled with stars, the old man and the rabbit in full bloom on the ripened moon. The breeze whispered through the palm fronds and branches creaked and groaned. Sparks of green and gold seemed to travel along the veins of the leaves. He rubbed his eyes, but the sparks were still there, evidence of the taw saun's power. Night birds called and batwings shushed between him and the mystical starlight. Moisture from the river fell like dew on his skin and dampened his clothing. He dozed.

Eventually, stirring under the vizier's kitchens woke him. Someone stepped cautiously through the sleepers there and out into the night where the moonlight caught her profile. Daw Ma Sanda.

He hauled himself upright on a tree and stepped out to reveal himself. Daw Ma Sanda fell back a step, her hand to her throat.

"Aung? Is that you?" Her voice carried more than he wanted it to.

He stepped closer, nodded, and held his finger

to his lips. He motioned toward the small creek where they had talked previously.

When they reached the spot where they'd enjoyed the sun, Daw Ma Sanda caught his arm. "How did you know I would step out at night?"

He smiled down at her, feeling the loss of their old love. "That was no mystery. You are of an age with me. It means we do not make it a full night without a trip to the latrine." He shrugged. "I thought I would take a chance and wait for you."

She shook her head, her long hair loose around her shoulders, the moonlight catching in the silvered threads, but unlike the yoke thei's magic, with humans it just meant old age. "How long have you been waiting, then?"

He shrugged again. "A while."

"And where is your little friend?" Her back was rigid.

"Pardon me?" How could she possibly know of Yamin?

"Don't give me that innocent look, Aung." She crossed her arms over her chest. "It was described as an imp. One of your infernal nats, I'd say. How can a good man consort with something unholy? You should burn the lot of them."

Perhaps he'd made a mistake coming here. Daw Ma Sanda was no longer the person he'd thought he knew. But he needed information, clarification, and Daw Ma Sanda offered the only source he had.

"I do not consort with ill-natured beings. I

came tonight because I could not sleep for my questions."

She eyed him. "Well then. What are they?"

"Perhaps we should get comfortable." He motioned to the creek bank and the silver runnel of water. It would feel good on his aching feet. He settled himself on the grassy bank and dabbled his toes, waiting for her to follow. She left for a moment and then settled beside him to stare up at the stars. "The others are sleeping. So?"

He thought for a moment considering how to start. "When we last spoke, you mentioned your vizier and how he does not like the rumors of war. What more can you tell me of him?"

Daw Ma Sanda's gaze inspected him and then she looked at the stars again. "He does not like lives spent unnecessarily. He has served Bodawpaya for many years through all of his wars and has been a most faithful servant."

A good assessment that confirmed what he'd heard of the man. "Does his role include meeting with emissaries on behalf of the king?"

Her gaze snapped back to him. "Perhaps. Sometimes."

He looked away. "This next question is hard and I wish only your honest answer. Has he been meeting with emissaries of foreign powers? Your priests, for example? Does your vizier follow your beliefs?"

"How dare you suggest that a Christian would undermine the king!" Daw Ma Sanda went to scramble to her feet, but Aung snagged her wrists and held her in place.

"I said it would be a hard question. Please give me your answer."

"The priests are good men. They speak the word of God!"

"And, perhaps of other realms and other kings. Is that a possibility?"

She looked away, all her muscles straining, but finally she sighed. "He has met with emissaries, but he still follows the king's ways and Buddha. He has not yet found God."

How far to push it? She might just walk away. "Daw Ma Sanda, I am sorry to ask you such troubling questions, but is there any way that the vizier might plot with the foreigners?"

"Absolutely not!" But the fear in her voice said otherwise.

"Is that your fear for your livelihood, or the truth?"

She paused. "He would not. He is loyal to the king, regardless of his feelings. That is my assessment." Her finality cut off further conversation in that direction.

"All right, then. I have another area of questions. I need to know more about these rumors of the young queen-to-be."

"Aah. The rumors of her infidelity." She nodded and her tension eased.

So this was not so troubling to her. Was it possible that Daw Ma Sanda could prefer these questions because she was hiding something about the vizier? It was something to think upon.

"They are little rumors so far, as if no one wishes to believe. But regularly she sends messages in the morning and in the evening leaves the seclusion of the Queens' house to go for walks in the gardens. Often she is not back until night has fallen."

"Where does she go?"

Daw Ma Sanda shrugged. "Who can say? I've heard that she leaves upon the westward headed path."

"Has no one followed her? Has no one checked who she speaks to or sees?" He glanced at her sideways, assessing whether she was keeping something from him but, unlike when she spoke of the vizier, her gaze was open as she shook her head.

"The queens' maids say there have been discussions, but number one queen advised against it."

"That is a surprise, is it not?"

"I think it is sign that the king's first wife cares not that he brings a common girl into the royal enclosure. The girl is no threat to the crown prince's grandmother. Let the girl make a fool of the king."

Aung's thoughts ran in multiple directions. "Or the queen has, perhaps, another purpose? If the girl is the beauty all claim, perhaps she has captured the heart of someone beyond the king?"

Daw MaSanda's gaze widened. "Prince Bagyidaw? By all that is holy, that could be. The young man is known for his wandering eye."

"But would his mother allow it? Would she not want a better match for her son?"

This time she shook her head, her long fall of hair shimmering around her bare shoulders. "Bagyidaw has a Number One Wife. As number two wife, the girl would be not much more than number one wife's slave until Bagyidaw marries yet again."

Aung thought a moment. "What is number one queen's relationship like with the king?"

Daw Ma Sanda's laughter bubbled into the darkness like a hidden spring. "It has been a long time since he visited her apartments and I hear that she prefers it that way."

So ridiculing Bodawpaya by cuckolding him, or better yet, ridiculing him by ruining the wedding would work to her and her son's favor.

"What is it? By your face, you have reached a conclusion."

Aung shook his head. "It is a suspicion only." He caught her hands. "Until I have proof it should not be shared and neither should this conversation. Please."

She paused, then nodded. "Your questions send my mind racing, Aung. If what I think you are thinking is correct… What are we to do? What am I to do? A new king would want a new vizier."

And she would be as destitute as she had

feared.

"Take no hasty action, for this may not be the case. Let me finish my investigation, please."

"I said I would not say anything." In the moonlight she leaned against his shoulder just as she had done so long ago. "It is hard to believe I am older. Was it not just yesterday I was a new bride? And the day before that was it not we two planning our future together?"

"It was."

"I still cannot believe that you never married."

"I married the songs and my duties. All considered, it has been a good marriage and life."

Away, beyond the enclosure a distant cock crowed and a faint blush of color marred the darkness above the eastern wall.

"I should go," Aung said. "I have much to do today, for the pwe is day after tomorrow."

"Tomorrow, you mean," she murmured. Behind them stirring sounded from the vizier's palace. "And I should return to my duties."

She stood and left him, her slim form disappearing through the screen of trees as if she was a taw saun, and he wondered whether he would ever see her again, would ever again feel the warmth of her shoulder against his.

As he walked away, the sharp pain in his chest suggested he knew the answer.

Chapter 8

When he returned to the guesthouse the others were awake. Saya Lin and U Winna pulled Aung aside. "Where did you go this morning?"

"Out to clarify a few things that I need to further my investigation." He glanced up at their expectant faces, Saya Lin curious, U Winna still resentful. "What have you two done while I have investigated? Have you found a way to save our lives by healing the Min? Have you rewritten our stories without the garuda?"

Saya Lin opened his mouth as if to speak. Then his shoulders slumped and he went to the wicker basket that still sat aside from the others. U Winna shook his head and left to join the puppeteers readying breakfast of last night's rice and fish.

Saya Lin returned with the little Min cradled in his hands and settled on his haunches beside Aung's stool. The puppet still wore his thick ornately jeweled tabard and paso, but even with the crown, it could not hide the damage to the beautifully painted face, or the different wood holding the head in place. Saya Lin sighed heavily and shook his head. "It is not good. We used a plug of common teak to hold the head together and another to hold the head onto the body, but we cannot reanimate something that is no longer living. His puppeteer says the spirit has abandoned the wood and I believe him. Nai Thiha has lived with the Min all his life. When he was a boy, his father bathed him and the Min in the same water. His first grasp was to take the strings from his father's hands. The man is heartbroken. His wooden brother is gone. I cannot ask him to dance the travesty we have created. I'm not even certain the other yoke thei will perform with a piece of them missing."

"Then what are we to do, old friend? I can try to find the culprit who has destroyed our troupe, but you must help old U Winna to find a long-term solution."

Saya Lin nodded. "If there is one," he said glumly. "What will you do?"

Aung glanced in U Winna's direction and lowered his voice. "I mentioned the rumors of the bride-to-be's infidelity. She apparently sends messages into the city and then goes walking. No one knows where."

"Perhaps she walks to settle her nerves. Marrying a king will not be easy."

Which was the truth as far as it went. Life under Bodawpaya was increasingly rigid, and he herded huge numbers of peasants from the fields to labor on his mad construction of what was to be the largest temple to Buddha in the world. It was all part of his belief that he was *Maitreya*—the next Buddha. Given his temper, this was hard to believe, but it had led to him promoting Buddhism above all else, and that could not help but further anger the nats that had lived in this land far longer than Buddha had. No wonder the rains had not come. Perhaps that explained the taw saun's anger.

"The crown prince is old enough to assume the throne. What if he no longer wishes to wait?" Aung offered. "What if he wished the girl as his bride as a symbol of his ascendancy? It would undermine Bodawpaya and could lead to a coup."

Saya Lin's eyes widened and he hunched in closer. "But how would he do such a thing on his own?"

Aung shrugged. "He could work with his mother. That could explain the queen's girl seen near here. She could have damaged the puppet to stop the performance and stop the spirit blessings."

Saya Lin shook his head. "But would not the old queen lose much status if she became merely the king's grandmother? From what I hear, she likes being Number One Queen very much. I heard the prince had even taken his grandfather's side over the marriage. I do not think she is our culprit."

"But in palace intrigue, Bagyidaw's rumored stance could simply be a cover for his real intent. I need to learn who the girl meets with."

"After you left us last night, U Winna suggested that perhaps Thiri sends regular messages to her mother. That could explain it."

"Perhaps." Aung nodded. He looked at U Winna. How was he to broach the truth with the man once he discovered it?

"You upset him badly," Saya Lin murmured. "It was ill done, my friend. Have a care. He is tender with that part of his heart. She is his most cherished child."

Aung sighed. "I did not choose it. The tale was brought to my attention and anything that reflects on the marriage may reflect on the murder of the Min."

Saya Lin pursed his lips and shook his head. "I do not understand how you can say that. It is a wedding between a man and a woman."

"And that, Ko Saya Lin, overlooks that it is a marriage between a woman and a *king*. That changes everything." Aung used the honorific that meant brother and tapped his finger beside his nose. A cool breeze blew the scent of water through the door as if rain fell somewhere near. Perhaps it was a sign that his logic was correct. Perhaps he'd been wrong that angry nats withheld the rain and the people's prayers would be answered.

He bowed his head briefly in the direction of the coconut nat shrine above him in the house and sent a word of prayer to the king of nats. "I cannot explain it, but when I heard of the messages from the girl everything seemed to fit, though I do not know how. If it is Bagyidaw, then it is consistent with the taw saun's words that the culprit is a leader of men."

"You believe him then?"

Aung raised his brow at Saya Lin's question. "When we live with the yoke thei you would doubt the word of the nats?"

"They are a tricky lot. Think of Yamin. They can take pleasure in causing havoc and have been known to relish revenge for slights." Saya Lin raised his chin at the little one seated on his trunk kicking his heels and nibbling a few grains of rice.

"Odd. It is Yamin who has reminded me that the nats are beings I have learned to trust. It is something Bodawpaya should pay more attention to."

Saya Lin glanced over his shoulder. "Have a care, Aung. We are in his court."

Aung smiled. "But I am speaking to you, and softly."

Saya Lin nodded. "So what now, old friend? How do we overcome this? Do we leave the royal enclosure and make a run for the mountains, or do we find a way to honor the Great Nats and perform?"

Aung peered out from under the house to where the sun raised its head above the tops of the trees and long columns of light brought mist from the earth. The light breeze enlivened the bells on the palace eaves and their tinkling voices filled the gardens. Leaves clapped slowly in time and birds sang counterpoint. Under the vizier's palace

Daw Ma Sanda and her companions would be completing grinding the condiments for the great man's morning lahpet. It would be the same for each of the palaces in the royal enclosure, and yet somewhere there would be a difference. Somewhere a darkness dwelt as someone plotted the troupe's destruction.

That darkness filled the tree shadows all around them, right up to the enclosure walls. There was no way out.

"I think escape is now beyond us, so we must find a way to perform. The wedding pwe will begin tonight with the court dancers. We should think on our alternatives."

He stood up and stretched and Saya Lin did the same.

"Wait! Wait!" Yamin said leaping off his basket where he'd clearly been eavesdropping. He trotted over to them. "If it is the prince, couldn't we find out by following the young queen?" The two old men looked at each other and then back at him.

"It is a possibility," Aung said considering, though it placed them in danger if they were caught.

"Then we should do it, shouldn't we?" Yamin rocked on the balls of his feet, positively vibrating with the need to go.

It could give them the answer, but even if they had it, Aung was uncertain the knowledge would help them. It would simply let them know from what direction the axe fell. But at least they might understand what was happening and why. With an awareness that came with years of mutual labor Saya Lin and he met each other's gaze.

"Perhaps I will keep watch for the messenger the girl sends," Aung said. "That may solve our mystery of who murdered our little king. If not, then I will follow her when she leaves on her walk this evening."

"How many years have we worked together to preserve this troupe?" Saya Lin asked.

"Almost two lifetimes," Aung replied sadly. A pittance compared to the millennia of the nats. And now it all was ending.

CHAPTER 9

Of course Yamin tagged along after the old singer when he left the house. *He* wasn't about to be left behind just when things were getting good. Besides, it had been *his* idea, and a very good one if he did say so himself. He looked up at the singer who hobbled through the tree apparently as quietly as he could.

It wasn't very good, for branches cracked under his stumbling feet and leaves swayed and thrashed as he passed. Altogether unacceptable when you are trying to be stealthy.

But being old had an advantage, too, for the old singer went unremarked as he passed through the gardens, almost as if age made one almost invisible. Interesting. Just beyond a screen of flame trees, their crowns ablaze with vivid blooms, the old man settled in the shade and leaned back against the trunk to wait.

Beyond the trees and past the bougainvillea, stood the lesser queens' teak palace. The servants huddled in the shade underneath. The high-pitched wail of a hne and the reverberating notes of a gong circle came plaintively out the window. The air still carried the last vestige of night coolness, but the rising sun would soon parch it away, just as it parched the moisture from the tree. Or old wood. Yamin rubbed his arms and felt the years in his flesh. Like drifts of old blood the tree's faded crimson blossoms littered the cracked earth. Now that was an unhappy thought and entirely *not* what he should be thinking.

The old singer shifted as if the earth was hard under his haunches.

"So? Has the new queen sent her messenger yet?" Yamin stepped out of the shadows to stand beside the singer and peer out at the palace.

"A few servants have entered carrying trays, but no one has exited—yet."

Yamin flopped on his stomach his head in his hands. "So I saw. I guess we wait, then."

The singer nodded down at him. "You followed me again. Tell me, why is this investigation so important to you? You are a child, a boy, and must have many more exciting things to do than accompany an old man."

Yamin rolled over onto his back, and held his hands up against the sky making animal forms against the blue. "In fact I am old. Much older than you, and my wood tells me that this is important to do. After all, it was Min who was killed and garuda is still missing and likely destroyed. I, myself, don't think we will find him. He does not give up his feathers so easily. So it could be any of us next and I would not like to see that happen."

The old man's thick grey brows rose as if he

had expected Yamin to always be young and frivolous. As if that was all he was capable of. Darn human opinions—they got stuck and there was no way to change them.

"Tell me, Yamin. Will the yoke thei perform without the Min?"

He wiggled his toes and fingers in the air, and thought about the question. Then he shook his head. "I don't know. The others—the great ones aren't going to tell me, now are they? I'm simply the page to them—and the others—the puppeteers." He sighed and rolled up to sitting. The old singer had given more time to him than anyone had in a very long time. "Tell me, Master Singer? What do you think of me? Am I just trouble as Mintha says? Am I only a burden as Minthamee tells me from time to time? She likes my jokes—but only sometimes."

Again the old man's gaze flickered as if he had not expected such a question. Then he scratched his chin.

"In truth? Often you seem no more than a foolish child, but a burden? No. Your constant pranks and jibes can grow tiresome sometimes, though. They wear on a person."

Yamin leapt up to pace around the trunk of the flame tree. He stopped on the other side of the old man. "But it is what they expect of me! I don't understand. Why is it that people expect you to act a certain way and then don't like you for it when you do?"

"A very good question, young man. And one I have no answer for. Perhaps people like to place each other in a box and expect them to stay there so that they get no unwanted surprises."

"And once you are in that box, they won't let you out again." Yamin plopped down and sighed as he ran his fingers through the dusty earth. But feeling sorry for oneself never got one anywhere. He looked up at the Singer. There was concern in the old man's gaze.

"It occurs to me, Master Singer, that we may sit here all day and not know who is the messenger we seek. Would it not be better to be closer to the palace and hear when the new queen sends the messenger forth?"

"Indeed it would be better. It would be better still if I could ask the young queen-to-be to notify me when she sends her messenger, but I doubt that will happen. We cannot go closer for we would be seen and we dare not show our intentions."

Yamin leapt to his feet and rubbed his hands together. "*You* might be seen, but *I* would not be. I, myself, am small and can be very quiet." He darted from Aung's shadow and out between the trees.

"Yamin wait! You'll be seen!"

He turned back and grinned and then plunged into the tall grass beside the queen's pavilion.

~~~

Grass barely rustled as if there was a slight breeze and then the little page was gone. For all
~~~

his annoying qualities, there was more depth to the little one than Aung had imagined. He would never have thought the puppet would volunteer for this duty.

Aung held his breath and sank back to his vantage point, waiting for the outcry that would mean Yamin had been discovered. Minutes ticked by and there were only the voices of the serving women and the buzzing of flies that had grown fat and round on dung left on the roads of the enclosure. The minutes turned to hours. As the morning spent itself, men and women came and went and still there was no sign of Yamin or any indication of the messenger. Perhaps this venture was in vain? With the pwe tonight and tomorrow, they were running out of time.

It was in the sweltering hour before noon, when all wise men and women were safe under the houses away from the glare of the sun, when a small motion in the grass brought Aung upright. A sparse moment later a puffing Yamin appeared and raised his arms in triumph. He swaggered up to Aung and plopped down on the ground.

"I like a job well done and this one is complete. The young queen-to-be's messenger is leaving as we speak." He peered over his shoulder as a young woman stepped down from the palace stair, looked left and right and then proceeded down the main path.

"See there? I saw the queen-to-be pass a message to her. By the stains on her hands, I think she brings flowers to the queens' bowers." Yamin swiped his hands at a task complete.

Aung struggled up to standing, his knees and back protesting. "You're sure it is her?"

Yamin nodded cockily. "As sure as I am that you stand before me."

"Then I bid you goodbye and beg you to return to the others. Following the messenger falls to me." He left Yamin and stepped out of the trees and onto the path with the messenger already invisible ahead of him on the curving path.

With the sun beating down, the shadows were hard black and the sunlight was blinding. Aung hobbled down the trail occasionally catching sight of the young woman. She was slight as a rice sheaf, barely more than a child, with black hair tied back with a strip of blue cloth and a floral longyi that could have been Daw Ma Sanda's except the young woman's was much newer and less faded.

Surprisingly, the girl did not step off the path. Instead, she followed it as it met wider roads that grew in importance like a river flowing away from the pool of the king and his nobles. Still, though the pathways met, there were few about at this hour. The young woman reached the walls of the royal enclosure, spoke with the guards and was allowed through the tunnel into Amarapura.

Aung sped up his pace, for he dared not lose sight of the girl in the city streets. He rushed up to the soldiers.

"I am Aung Aung of the royal puppeteers. I

need to purchase supplies in the city."

The sleepy-eyed guard narrowed his gaze. "At this hour? Why not send a courier instead of going in this heat, grandfather?"

"Some things are better done yourself," he snapped. Just let him get through. Every second counted.

Finally, the guard nodded him toward the tunnel.

Aung almost fell as he rushed through the shadows. The fetid moat beyond the walls steamed in the sun. Aung held his breath. Where? Where was the messenger?

Praise Buddha, the heat had kept the worst of the press of city people at home. Ahead a figure in a blue longyi turned down a side road from the large boulevard that edged the far side of the moat.

Aung rushed after her into a narrow street lined with stilted teak houses. Ahead a monastery turned round windows onto the street, the sound of chanting filling the sun-beaten pathway. Children played under the houses in the care of their dozing mothers and fathers. The scent of lahpet and grilled fish sent his stomach growling. A silver stupa pushed up through the houses, surrounded by smaller, white-washed stupa and a nat kadaw garlanded with orange flowers. Incense burned in front of the nat kadaw, uncoiling fragrance into the blue sky.

Far ahead the hurrying figure of the messenger turned down another side street. Aung rushed to keep up.

And found himself on a weaver's street. Lines were strung head-high across the street hung with long, silken skeins of thread dyed vivid colors of red and blue and green and yellow. Those threads would be used to weave the colorful paso and other garments of the wealthy merchants and nobles.

The pungent scents of dye filled the air and curdled his nostrils. The voices of the weavers and the thunk and clack of their looms sounded lazily from the shadows under the teak houses. The long threads shifted and trembled in a slight wind and blocked his view ahead.

He ducked through the first line of threads. They closed behind him, but there were more ahead and only more teak houses to either side. The caustic stench of dye and the scent of rice water stung his eyes. The sun drove down on his head and sweat filmed his eyes. His breath came too fast and his heart pounded too hard.

He stumbled and caught the planks of a building, felt his knees fold like old wood, and then he was falling. The parched earth reached up for him. He found himself trapped on his back between a house pole and a large pottery cistern of water, his legs and arms working like an upended turtle. Above there was only the cruel eye of the sun peering down.

"Grandfather! Are you hurt?" A melodious voice came from right near his head. Then strong hands caught his shoulders and helped right him. The owner of the hands came around the pole. A woman, round faced and round bodied and heavy with child. She wore her hair as Daw Ma Sanda did, coiled up behind her head. White thannaka paste protected her face and the backs of her arms. Her hands were stained red.

"I think…I think I am well," he said, though his head swam. He tested each limb. He had skinned his shoulders somehow and blood seeped through the arms of his Indian tunic, but otherwise he was simply embarrassed. "I fear the sun was too much for me."

"Let me get you a cup of water," the woman said and used a gourd ladle to scoop him a cool drink from the cistern. He sucked it back and she refilled it. He drank more slowly this time.

"Do you need food?"

She must think him a beggar; he waved her off. "I must be going. Truly. There is someone I must find."

But what hope did he have now? He had already lost sight of the messenger and in the time since he had fallen, the girl could be anywhere. He sighed and staggered up. "*Mingala ba*. Bless you for your kindness. I fear my delay has made my errand useless."

He bowed and held his palms together breast-high in thanks. Then he left her. Shoulders heavy with failure, he turned towards the royal enclosure and home. He had one more chance to find the

truth and expose the prince's plotting.
Only one.

CHAPTER 10

The day faded to a somnolent, breezeless afternoon under a burning sun. Cicadas hummed. The creeks faded and dried to cracked mud. The bells on the eaves of the tall teak noble houses and the golden umbrella on the royal palaces all hung mute under the bowl of unending blue sky. Even the noble and royal voices were subdued, so that the sounds of the city, market women, tea *wallahs*, the chip, chip, chip of the stone masons filled the afternoon like moans and the markers for the passing of seconds as Aung once more waited in the shade of the flame tree. The day was ending after an insufferable afternoon, and as yet there was no sign of U Winna's daughter leaving for her assignation.

The dusty sweet scent of thannaka spiked the air. The queen's Arakanese slaves must be grinding the scented wood for their noble betters. The scent of fish roasting over a fire and of sweet curry leaves and pumpkin made his stomach growl. He should have eaten before he came, but the handful of white rice he had grabbed from the lunchtime pot would have to do. He could not afford to miss the young queen-to-be's departure.

He had returned to the guesthouse through the middle of the day, but had refused to answer any of the questions tossed his way. The burden of disaster weighed heavy on his shoulders, just as it did now. If they could just learn who had caused the destruction of Min, then they might protect themselves from the disaster brooding in the royal enclosure.

When he'd returned, the aching silence under the guesthouse had said that the puppeteers and Saya Lin had been no more successful than him in reclaiming garuda or finding a way that they might perform. The time of the yoke thei was ending and the troupe would be put to death at the pleasure of the king, unless they could find who had done this to them and named the perpetrator. If they uncovered plots within the royal enclosure, they might even gain the king's favor—at least for a little while. Bodawpaya might even suffer them to leave Amarapura.

Even if he stripped the royal patronage from them, with U Winna's skills as a manager and the yoke thei cooperation, they still might have a livelihood.

He had tossed and turned through the heat of the day and then, as the shadows had lengthened, he had returned here. So far he had nothing to show for it except more hunger pangs. He yearned for the comfort of his bed, his eyes for the light and the smiles of old friends. The low, indistinguishable voices of the serving women and the soft laughter of the queens and royal concubines seemed to ruffle his skin, like the breeze. Gradually, the evening hummed around him in a cicada voice that demanded his attention. He straightened.

The grass beside him stirred when there was no wind, and Yamin poked his head out from between the stalks. "Here again, I see. I thought so." He dragged a bag almost as big he was out of the grass. "I brought you something." He dropped it at Aung's knee and the bag opened released the scent of rice, pumpkin, and lake prawns.

Aung's mouth watered and he pulled open the bag. "Thank you! What brought you to think of this kindness?"

Yamin shrugged, his pony tails wagging on his head. "I thought your noisy stomach might have been why you lost the girl this morning. Besides, you need your strength." He sank down beside Aung, nibbling on a rice kernel. "So she hasn't left yet."

Aung sighed around the delicious nutty flavor of the rice and the succulence of a prawn. "She may not. Perhaps her message today was her final farewell—if her lover is a commoner."

"We are doomed then," Yamin said sadly.

The sentiment echoed Aung's morbid thoughts. "There is still time. It is not yet dusk."

"You put much store in your friend's rumors," Yamin said.

"I have little more to go on. This is a topsy

turvy case, Young Page. I find myself grasping at shadows and spirits, and I fear the Great Nats have deserted us. They do not bring the rains to help a country, so how can I expect them to help us?" He glanced down at Yamin. "I had hoped that they would help because you are nats, too."

Yamin sighed uncharacteristically. "Perhaps they don't help because we are little enough, too. The least of spirits, not even a complete tree anymore." His eyes glistened as if he was close to crying.

Aung straightened. For the page to cry would be as if the very world was ending. Yamin, his laughter, kept the world young. Was this what the world had come to? He had to do something. Perhaps sitting here was wasting what little time they had to escape or to plan some means of still performing for the king.

He wobbled up to standing, his body stiff from his morning's labor, his bruised sides aching from his fall. "Perhaps…" he began.

Yamin pointed at the palace.

The gray pall of dusk had filled the gardens, the last angled sunlight catching in the city dust that rose over the royal enclosure's western walls. The queens' palace had become a place of unpleasant angles and shadows, yawning windows and doorways giving onto deeper darkness within. The sweetness of incense and perfume rose with the wood smoke of the dinner fires beneath the building, but at one side of the building a slim female figure stood at an open doorway. She checked over her shoulder and then cast her gaze around the garden.

Even from this distance it was clear she was a beauty. Thick dark hair coiled ornately around her brow, while the back fell luxuriantly over her shoulders. High arched brows and high cheekbones framed large almond eyes and a perfect full mouth made a pale pink bow. She wore not a queen's finery, but a simple servant's longyi of bright yellow floral cotton and a simple white blouse. Barefoot, she slipped down the stairs and in amidst the trees not far from Aung.

"She did not see us," Yamin said.

"Likely she looked for soldiers. She did not see what she did not expect," Aung whispered. He eased away from the tree and onto a narrow woodland path that the young woman followed. Yamin disappeared into the grass.

The falling sun had silenced the comforting daytime cries of peacock and doves. They had been replaced by the rattle and twang of the pwe orchestra as they prepared for the performance that would run all night and next day. The golden glow of the stupa spires of the Sagaing hills had died away to grey as he surreptitiously followed the girl away from the music and the ornately carved royal buildings. Tomorrow was the planned performance of the yoke thei. Tomorrow they would either be exposed as an incomplete puppet troupe, or they would expose the betrayer of the king.

In the barely lessened heat, the tulip tree branches hung low over the path and heavy with crimson blooms gone grey in the dusk, the astringent scent of eucalyptus and the spiciness of teak pervaded everything.

The darkness ate his vision as the candle glow from the women's teak-latticed windows and the cooking fires fell behind. How did he expect to see anything or anyone like this? With his old man's eyesight he was half blind even in high daylight. The stars strung across the heavens in a blanket of white, truncated by the occasional cloud. Around him, nat breath and voices filled the murmur of the leaves and the soft liquid music that came from the trickling streams. Perhaps the taw saun's nature nats came to support him in finding the truth. He hoped.

A night-darkened cloud floated across the stars and he hesitated. The trees shifted and moved as if in an unfelt strong wind and the scent of water increased and carried with it the fresh perfume of thannaka.

The woman could not be far ahead. He squinted into the darkness and made out her slight figure. She kept moving, making it difficult to follow for she did not make allowances for an old man's slower hobble. She moved swiftly across the lawns and through the park-like trees as if she had done it many times. His old man's legs did not take well to the uneven lawn, or the prospect of a short leap over a creek. Still, he managed to not fall or catch her attention.

Eventually she came to a torch-lit path that served as the main processional road from the king's palace to the royal enclosure's main gate. This road was reserved for royalty, or the visits of the king's religious advisors from the temple of the Mahamuni Buddha that had recently been stolen from Arakan. For the girl to come this way, she must truly be meeting Prince Bagyidaw.

Aung's stomach twisted. Revealing such a thing might save their lives today, but it would also make an evil enemy of the future king. He shivered, but kept following, for the truth was worth something. Did it equate to his troupe-mates' lives? He might be long dead by the time Bagyidaw was king, but Thura and the other apprentices were young—they had their whole lives before them.

He quickened his pace—until a hand caught his shoulder.

"Who are you? What are you doing here?" asked a young soldier. "This is a road only for members of the royal household."

Aung glanced to where the girl disappeared briefly in the darkness between each torch. The path curved through the trees. If he lost sight of her he would not find her again and all was truly lost.

"I am sorry. I did not know. I am one of the workers of U Winna's yoke thei troupe. I was going to market for offerings for our performance." Hopefully the ruse would work again.

He faced the soldier's inspection, and knew he failed by the slight curl of the man's upper lip. To be expected, he supposed when he wore an old man's faded paso and tunic, and his remaining hair sprouted like wild grass through the loose folds of his farmer's turban.

"There are other roads and gates. See you use them after tonight. Do not go wandering in the royal enclosure. The king prefers his privacy."

As if he didn't know that. But Aung bowed low, his palms pressed together in front of his face in an unreasonable show of respect to a youth. Let the man think he was Aung's better if it would gain him freedom sooner.

"Go on with you, then."

Aung scurried away as fast as his legs would take him around the curve in time to see the girl reappear again, then disappear into another space between torches—and not come out again.

The road was empty.

He stopped dead in the road, inhaling the reek of mud from the king's lake, the long dry season having stolen most of the shallow water out from under the king's barges. Where was she? The air had the electric feeling of the nats' nearness—and foreboding.

She must have stepped off the path and struck out into the trees again, but he did not know in which direction.

"This way. Quickly!" Yamin's voice hissed in the darkness to his left. "I thought that soldier would arrest you and I, myself, would have to do this."

Aung checked behind for the soldier and then stepped down amid the trees. There she was, a distant figure ducking between the tree trunks and following the long line of the enclosure walls.

A small hand found his. "Come."

~~~

The old singer's skin was like paper, his fingers mostly bone, but he clung to Yamin's hand as if he was a blind man.

Yamin led him through the trees by the gleam of the insects and the slight iridescence of the edges of leaves. This was the taw saun's forest, after all. The woman picked her way through the trees and hedges until she reached a secluded bower of bougainvillea that had been laced over a stone seat beside the tinkling flow of the creek. She ducked inside.

"Did you see?" Yamin asked.

He felt the old man nod and led him closer. Soft voices floated on the dusky air.

"I cannot believe the time is almost here. What are we to do?" said a soft female voice that must be the young queen.

"The marriage will not happen. I have seen to it," whispered a male voice.
~~~

Had he heard it before? Yamin cocked his head. The trouble was most humans sounded uncommonly like one another. It must take another human to tell them apart.

"But there has been no outcry. The king is determined." The girl's plaintive cry. "Only yesterday he sent gold and ruby earrings for me to wear in the ceremony. The queens were so jealous that I feared for my life."

"All will be fine, Thiri. Just trust in me. Tomorrow the king will believe that the marriage is inauspicious. He may not sanction the nats, but he will not wish to marry without the blessings the people expect." The voice was assured—the kind that belonged to a man who was the master in all he did.

"The puppet?" she asked.

"It was well done—beyond their power to undo." A little gloating and a little regret came through.

But…

"But that's…" Yamin started, full voiced.

The old singer slapped a hand over his mouth. The voices went silent as Yamin was dragged back into darkness.

A dark figure stepped from the bower. "Who's there?"

The old singer stood frozen, for even his old eyes must recognize the portly figure. No vizier, no city man and no Prince of Burma, the human leader of the puppet troupe stood draped in darkness.

"U Winna? How can this be? Surely this is a joke you play on me." The old singer motioned Yamin to stay concealed and then stepped forward. "Tell me this is all a mistake."

The girl stepped from the bower—a pretty enough little thing but no match for Minthamee's beauty—and the puppet troupe leader pulled her to his side. His face had set into protective resolve that must be what a father looked like. He was angry, too—not someone Yamin would trust at all!

"How could it be any other way?" the troupe leader said. "The king steals my precious daughter without even so much as a bride's purse. It's supposed to be enough that she becomes his toy and the slave of his den of she-monster queens. How is a father who loves his daughter to stand for that?"

"But you killed the Min!" Yamin couldn't hold it in any longer. He leapt to the old singer's side and grabbed his hand.

The troupe leader scowled down at him and up at the singer. "I see your loyalty rests with bits of wood, not with the lives of men."

"But your actions place all at risk!" The old singer finally found his voice, but his shoulders had sagged with his friend's betrayal. The old man must have trusted him a great deal. "The king's wrath will come down on all of us—you included!"

"Not so." The troupe leader shook his head. "Thiri and I are leaving. Let you and the others lose your heads—if you are foolish enough to stay."

"But the troupe. Saya Lin, the others, the yoke thei. You would abandon us all?" the old singer asked.

"For my daughter, yes. What do I care for bits of wood?"

"We are not just bits of wood!" Yamin stepped up to him and kicked his shin.

The troupe leader kicked him back and sent Yamin tumbling head over heels in the rough grass. He picked himself up, checking for damage and dusted off his clothes. Then he marched right back to the singer's side.

"That was poorly done," the old singer said. "Are you all right, Yamin?"

He nodded and stuck out his tongue at the other man.

The troupe leader rolled his eyes. "Fools all of you, running around examining all your suspects. I did what had to be done. I killed the king I could get my hands on. I broke his neck and shattered his head. If only it had been Bodawpaya's!" His hands fisted, but then he caught his daughter's hand and turned to go.

"You can't do this," the old singer said.

"You cannot stop me, old man."

"Stay, U Winna. We're your friends. Together we'll find some way to appease the king and the marriage will go ahead."

"There can be no marriage if my daughter is not here. And as for appeasing the king—I would like to see you try. Perhaps this fool of yours can wear the king's robes. His decisions will surely be as enlightened as Bodawpaya's."

The troupe leader led his daughter away.

"Think carefully, U Winna," Aung called softly. "When the king discovers your daughter missing he will search the city."

"Then we will not be in the city."

"He will search the countryside, too. And when he finds you, you know what he will do."

"Then perhaps we'll come back to haunt him as one of those nats of yours."

"Father are you sure?" the girl's worried voice floated back, but the troupe master's reply was lost in the darkness and whispers of the night-bound leaves. There was every chance that the gate guard would not recognize the girl, and the troupe leader would do exactly what he said.

"What do we do?" Yamin asked.

"Find a way to save ourselves. The man has made up his mind to seek another fate."

"I, myself, am not a fool, I hope you know. And I am not just some piece of wood, either," Yamin said. "Everyone underestimates me." He reached up for the old singer's dry hand. "Except maybe you."

Chapter 11

The nighttime garden pulsed around Aung as he stood with Yamin. The air felt thick with lightning as if the nats were near. As if the Great Ones settled U Winna's fate and placed a blessing on the small page's words. Overhead the star-crossed heavens had dimmed beneath a layer of gossamer cloud, but southward—southward where the Andaman winds blew came huge cloud towers like a fleet of foreign ships that would ravage Burmese lands.

He caught Yamin and lifted the little page up to his shoulder. "We must get back to the others. You are brilliant once again, Master Page."

Burdened by the grief of U Winna's betrayal, he hurried through the perfumed trees, to the guesthouse. When he arrived, the area under the house was in turmoil around the cook fire, the yoke thei milling to one side. U Winna had been missed and the troupe's first performance was perilously close. Saya Lin was trying to calm the fear and outrage.

"Aung!" Saya Lin shoved through the others when Aung stepped into the firelight. "You came back! Where is U Winna?"

Aung set Yamin down to scamper over to the other yoke thei. "Was there ever any doubt that I would return? Have I not come back every other time?"

Saya Lin pulled him aside. "There was a rumor that you and U Winna escaped together. The troupe's purse is missing—unless he, too, is coming back again?"

Sighing, Aung shook his head. "That will not be happening. He is gone, along with his daughter."

"And all our funds." Saya Lin's legs folded under him and he sank to the earth. Aung crouched next to him and told what he had learned as the other puppeteers and musicians crowded around.

Saya Lin covered his face with his hands. "It is over, then. Garuda's absence we might survive, but we cannot perform without the Min, and the king will believe that we willingly killed him in effigy. With the loss of his bride I doubt his anger will know any bounds. Perhaps we should just turn ourselves in."

The troupe members' murmurs rose in argument until Aung held up a hand. "Hold! Yamin and I have a plan. We discussed it on the path home. U Winna himself suggested it in jest, but I believe it can be our salvation."

~~~

The next dawn filled the skies with the rouge of a harlot's cheeks, as the puppeteers and yoke
~~~

thei completed their final practice of their new performance. No one had slept the night away. Aung had composed new songs. The musicians had revised their music. Saya Lin and the puppeteers, with the surprising assistance of Yamin, had convinced the other puppets that the Min would want them to carry on without him.

As the afternoon faded to evening, servants arrived to help them carry their equipment to the puppet stage erected in the royal pavilion. The puppeteers jealously guarded their small charges, but the assistance was needed for the mighty gong circle of metal discs and the five-foot-long dragon drum suspended from the belly of its snarling dragon-shaped scaffold.

They arrived early at the pavilion, for the puppeteers were determined to inspect the stage to ensure no more disasters were forthcoming. They checked the slope of the stage—a coconut rolled precisely three times before coming to rest. The curtain painted with the Burmese countryside was hung perfectly straight behind the stage and the walkway used by the puppeteers was the exact height to allow them to work the puppets correctly from above. A silk cushion had been laid in each wing of the stage where Aung and young Thura would sit to sing their songs. All was as it should be.

The royal pavilion's teak platform was inlaid with mirrors and precious stones. More wound up the mighty pillars that held up the high peaked roof with its dragon-shaped lintels. At one end, Bodawpaya's lion throne sat on its platform above the seating area of the rest of the audience. Only the stage was set higher than the king's head—a singular honor enjoyed solely by the puppet troupe.

"You realize this may be our last performance." Saya Lin had sidled up beside Aung beside the stage as they studied the rich draperies and golden umbrella over the king's throne. "Bodawpaya could be insulted by your song, our dance, by anything. He is a fickle king." He shook his head.

Aung nodded. "But he may surprise us. He is a man beset by problems. That is the thing with life: one never knows what will bring about its ending. Let us pray that the spirits see our efforts positively. Perhaps that will offset the king's fickle humor."

Aung raised his chin. "Look, the royal musicians have arrived. The king will not be far behind."

Nobles and notables filed in to take their seats on the floor's bamboo matting. The vizier in his silver headdress stepped onto the lowest step of the king's dais. The musicians began to play. The wail of the hne, the rich tremulous purr of the gong circle, the roll of the king's drums filled the pavilion and Aung felt a moment of panic. Had he led Saya Lin and the others astray? Would they have been better to attempt escape like U Winna?

The drums rolled again, and along the path through the garden strode a dozen ferocious-looking soldiers followed by a gold-clad Bodawpaya with Arakanese slaves holding a seven-tiered golden umbrella above him. Behind him came a phalanx of more fierce guards, spears held high and swords at the belts of their leather armor. Small bells tinkled softly from the umbrella.

Bodawpaya was a tall man with broad shoulders that had wielded the mighty sword that had gained him his throne from his brothers, fratricide being common in the Konbaung Dynasty. But years of good living had taken their toll: not even the drape of his crimson and gold paso and vest could hide the ample proportions of his belly, nor how he rolled when he walked. With his golden turban held high, he marched up the stair to the pavilion and strode imperiously through his nobles to the dais. He climbed the stairs and sat down firmly in his golden throne. His round face was flushed, his mouth down-turned more in the manner of a man who has just done battle, than of a man once more going to the pleasures of the marriage bed. A ruby on his forehead stared out like a vengeful red eye.

This was the man who had constant skirmishes with Siam, who had conquered Arakan, who had united a kingdom and made Buddhism the state religion. Of course, he had also outlawed the nats—difficult to do when the nats' images stood at every Buddhist temple.

But he was also a king under siege.

To the west, the Europeans were one-by-one taking control of the Mogul kingdoms, their latest attention turned on Manipur, the kingdom of the king's cousin. If Manipur fell, the foreigners would be at his gates far worse than they already were along the coast. Perhaps this marriage was a way to forget, for the moment, the troubles he faced. To lose them in the foolish pleasures of youth. Aung could almost relate and feel sorry for the man if his own fate was not so firmly linked to the king's humor.

Then the soldiers shifted forward and the vizier stepped down from the platform around the king's dias to meet them. He caught the arm of the person the soldiers escorted. A woman. No, a girl.

Though Aung had not seen her close up, nor in full daylight, it was clearly Thiri. He closed his eyes and said a prayer to guide U Winna's soul through the terrors and uncertainties of the newly dead. Certainly that had to be his fate. And partially it was Aung's fault for perhaps he could have stopped U Winna if he had been more clear-sighted in his investigation. The facts had been before him all along and he had refused to see U Winna as a suspect, just as Yamin said no one saw him as he truly was. His expectations had blinded him.

He looked back to U Winna's daughter. The girl was lovely, with skin like translucent celadon porcelain and hair as thick, dark and luxuriant as the deeps of night. Her gold and red longyi and tunic covered her demurely from throat to ankle, but served to only emphasize the loveliness of her figure. The vizier led her to a spot at the foot of the dais, beneath the lowest of the queens who stood on a raised platform to one side. She folded her legs gracefully beneath her and turned her face toward the stage.

Her gaze met Aung's and for a moment he forgot to breathe at the bleak world-weariness and grief filling her eyes. He looked away. How could one so young know all of the world's ills?

"The king knows!" Beside Aung, Saya Lin's voice threatened to break.

Aung caught his arm and pulled him behind the stage where the puppeteers huddled, waiting for their performance. "He knows U Winna left and tried to steal his daughter. He knows nothing of our issues. Now get the puppeteers and yoke thei ready." He cast around at the frightened troupe who fussed over the puppets and over Yamin most of all. "Thura, take your seat. Everyone, get ready. This must be our best performance ever." Little Yamin caught his eye and grinned as if he was enjoying the attention.

With Thura's help, Aung climbed into his seat, while the grand vizier formally announced the nuptials of the grandfather king—Bodawpaya and Thiri of Amarapura. They did not say her father's name. Aung peeked out from beyond the curtain.

The girl slumped where she sat, her gaze locked on the stage as if she dared not look elsewhere.

The court musicians stopped their playing. The rill of the gongs faded to a silence and left behind a gap in the world—perhaps one of the holy places the nats preferred. The king's edicts could not make the old ways simply go away. Bodawpaya needed to learn that and revise his expectations.

The high-pitched hne of the puppet musicians rose in a cry to the heavens. Up and up it spiraled as the yoke thei votaress danced onto the stage. The small female nat was clad in red, her dark hair bound to her head by a crimson sash. She danced perfectly, like a human dancer would, the magical silver strings in her hair making her one with her puppeteer.

Gracefully, she bowed to the nats of the four directions, offering to each her bowl of rice, banana and coconut. Then she set the bowl down in the corner of the stage and bowed to the king, before backing off the stage.

The music changed. The hne ended its plaintive call. The gongs shivered and then the drum unleashed a roll as the alchemist leapt onto the stage. The queens gasped as he leapt, tossed his wand in the air and caught it again. He, too, made offerings to the spirits.

The alchemist caused a small explosion and disappeared from the stage in the puff of smoke. Aung cleared his throat of cordite for here was where his work began. With the light shiver of the gong circle and the rising wail of the hne, Yamin tumbled onto the stage and stopped to peer out at the audience. He was a wayward little soul, but so much this night depended upon him.

In his small boy's pantaloons, he rocked on the balls of his feet and then opened his mouth. Aung began to sing Yamin's verse that emphasized his foolishness and youth even though he was tasked with arranging everything for the king's arrival. He chased imaginary butterflies across the stage, pretended he was an elephant to gales of laughter amid the queens, the royal children and noble crowd. Even Bodawpaya smiled and nodded. So—they were loosening his anger. That was good.

Yamin bounded off stage and was replaced by white-clad Minthamee and her Mintha, the princess and prince. They danced gracefully together arms swooping and twining as Aung sang their songs of love to each other.

A clash of the gongs and Mintha hurried Minthamee off the stage. Another clash of gongs and a roll of drums and the hne took up a processional wail. Saya Lin poked his head past the curtain looked anxiously at Aung for this was the moment where they varied from their usual performance.

The Min's procession entered the stage across from Aung. First came the Royal Ministers, and the governors of the cities and provinces. Aung readied himself, holding the new words of the hurriedly crafted song in his head. The procession stepped forward.

And Yamin stepped back on stage, this time instead of his usual pantaloons and vest, he wore overtop the striking jeweled robes and tabard of the Min. The robes were too long, dragging on the floor. The sleeves of the jacket hung ridiculously longer than his arms. The king's jeweled headdress perched jauntily between Yamin's two ponytails.

Stifled laughter rolled in from the audience and Bodawpaya leaned forward, no longer so grandfatherly.

The hne changed its tune to include some of Yamin's jaunty music and Aung picked up his song. He sang of time's passing and the waning of strength. He sang of the aching of bones and the dulling of eyesight. He sang of the pain of knowing life was waning. Yamin leapt from amidst the formal procession to thump down facing the king and audience. Aung closed his mouth and young Thura picked up the song for it needed his playful boy's voice. Pray let the boy get it right. His clear high voice rose into the night.

> "Except for me!
> I may be a grandfather king to my people,
> but in my heart I am still a boy.
> I make rules about the spirits
> Of war I make a toy."

Yamin/Min produced a sword from his side, almost as tall as he was. He lunged and stabbed at the sky as if to ward off the spirits. The gongs and drums shivered and all the while the procession of yoke thei nobles kept to their procession around the stage.

"I hold sway over all the land
From Andaman to the Kunming Mountains
From the people of Siam to the Manipuri.
I preserve my people safe from foreign ways
Or the foreigners will feel my fury!"

Yamin stabbed his sword at the sky again and danced through the noble procession as if he battled foes. Some of the procession fell, apparently lifeless, and he stood over them, waving his arms like a hero. Then he scratched under his royal turban almost knocking it off its precarious perch. The audience gave into their laughter and howled as he walked forward to the crowd where he scowled.

"The Burmese people
Toil for me
I want to bring, not war, but joy.
What better way than to marry a child
When, inside, I am but a boy!"

From the wings of the stage he pulled a handmaid. Saya Lin had worked magic, for with Yamin's touch, her handmaid's clothing stripped away to reveal a princess underneath. Arm in arm, Yamin and the handmaid led the stately procession off the stage. The gongs clashed. The drum roll ended. Thura collapsed across the stage from Aung as the monkey and the naga took the stage for rollicking fun.

Aung peered out at the audience. The nobles were still laughing and wiping their eyes. He chanced a look at the king. Usually Bodawpaya stayed stone faced at Aung's songs as if he barely tolerated them.

The king's hands rested on the lion throne's gilt arms. But he did not scowl. In fact, his lips curved in a smile. His gaze met Aung's. Then he gave a single small nod. Aung collapsed back into the wing of the stage and prepared himself for the rest of the night.

Songs and laughter blurred the remaining performance. When it was over, it took both Thura and Saya Lin to help Aung down from his perch at the side of the stage. Exhausted, he sank down on a stool in the hubbub behind the stage. The puppeteers were busy with the yoke thei, the little ones puffed up with the magic of their performance, so that it took care to ease them to return to the slumber of their wood in their cushioned baskets.

"I want to play! I want to play!" Yamin

shouted, his high-pitched voice like the gong of a bell.

"Hush! Do you want to bring the king's wrath down on us all? Are we not enough at risk as it is?" his puppeteer scolded.

Apparently the answer was "no," for Yamin leapt off his basket and scampered across the curtained enclosure to Aung. He still wore the king's ridiculously too-large robes with the hem pooled around his feet and the sleeves hiding his fingers.

"It went well, did it not? The king was appeased?"

Aung nodded. "It did and he was."

From overhead, on the roof of the royal pavilion, came a rumble and the sound that had troubled his dreams. Rain. Lightning flashed and thunder grumbled as a wet breeze blew through the trees and dampened the skin of royalty and nobles alike as they listened to the royal storyteller recounting Bodawpaya's mightiest deeds.

Aung struggled to his feet and peered out of the curtained enclosure behind the stage. Sheets of rain blew through the gardens. Leaves beat against branches as if they laughed. Water ran in swift rivulets across the parched ground to fill the stream beds and revive the water nats.

"Yamin, you must obey your puppeteer and go to bed. We must leave the royal enclosure tonight for we have another engagement."

"We do?" Yamin and Saya Lin said as one.

Aung nodded as he stepped out on the curtain and toward the rain. "At Popa. We must go to Popa and give thanks to the nats. All of them. The Great Ones answered our prayers and brought the rain, but it was the smallest of the small who saved us."

He bent down and shook Yamin's hand in front of everyone. "Thank you, Yamin. You proved yourself greater than many men."

Then Aung left them for the rain, letting the blessed liquid stream down his body. It filled his eyes and ears, and the gardens around him were transformed. Gone were the simple flame and tulips trees. Instead, handsome nats stepped from the tree trunks. Blue-skinned water nats rose from the streams, and their songs rose sweetly in the sound of rain on leaves. Aung joined them, for though a king may say he can command a country, truly it is only men who obey him. The nats hold their own sway.

A tug on his paso brought his gaze down from the drenching rain. Yamin. He had snuck out again. The page looked up at him with ancient eyes.

"What are you thinking about?" Yamin asked.

"U Winna. How I could not see past what I expected of him. As a result, I have lost a friend forever. I fear his life was forfeit to bring the rains." He shook his head. "Sad to lose a friend on a night when we should rejoice for the rain. Perhaps *we* shall be friends, Master Page."

Yamin gave a forceful nod and caught his

hand. "I, myself, shall be your partner. We shall solve mysteries together wherever we go.

Aung winced, then caught himself. The rest of his life spent corralling Yamin's youthful exuberance…

There were worse fates.

Karen L. Abrahamson writes mystery, fantasy and romantic fiction, and often likes to blend all three. She's best known for her *American Geological Survey* urban fantasy series that involves a race of beings who can change the world through their maps. Her first mystery novel, *Through Dark Water*, is set on the wild coast of British Columbia, Canada. Many of her stories take place in exotic settings around the world, in places she has lived or visited. She has a special affection for Myanmar/Burma, its people, nats and puppets.

Karen currently lives on the west coast of Canada with bald eagles, bears and the Pacific Ocean as neighbours.

~~~

Daniel Hand is British author and military historian. His work has appeared in *Swords and Sorcery Magazine*, *Myriad Lands: Volume 1* anthology (also from Guardbridge Books), and *Dekho!*, the magazine of the Burma Star Association. He is Chair of the International Writers Fellowship.
~~~

9 781911 486114